BACK TO MALACHI

BACK TO MALACHI

ROBERT J. CONLEY

DOUBLEDAY & COMPANY, INC.

GARDEN CITY, NEW YORK

1986

All of the characters in this book
are fictitious, and any resemblance
to actual persons, living or dead,
is purely coincidental.

Library of Congress Cataloging-in-Publication Data
Conley, Robert J.
    Back to Malachi.
    1. Cherokee Indians—Fiction.   I. Title.
PS3553.0494B3   1986   813'.54   86-8995
ISBN: 0-385-23698-0

for
Clu Gulager,
for
Don Coldsmith,
and for
Vicki Snell

AUTHOR'S NOTE

Some years ago while attempting research into the life of Ned Christie, I again ran across one of those references from a prominent "six-gun historian" (the phrase is Emmet Starr's.) which said, in effect, that Ned Christie, a full-blood Cherokee, was the worst outlaw ever to roam the Indian Territory. That is a bold statement. I tried in vain to find evidence to substantiate that claim. What I found were references to other "bad Cherokee outlaws," equally unsubstantiated. I have since, following further research and cogitation, written an article for *The Roundup*, "Cherokees 'On the Scout,'" which is an investigation of this phenomenon. In the meantime, I wrote *Back to Malachi* as a fictional exploration of the topic. Mose Pathkiller is not Ned Christie, though there are some similarities between the two and the manner of his death is an almost direct borrowing from the Ned Christie story.

BACK TO MALACHI

PROLOGUE

The rifle report filled the small cabin and left behind it a prolonged ringing that I thought would never leave my ears. It was the loudest noise I had ever heard in my life, and it left me stunned and immobile for what seemed like a long minute but must have been only a fraction of a second. Then I jumped up from my place at the table and was beside Mose at the window, shoving myself up against him to get a look outside. The horse was champing about and snorting, frightened at the sudden noise and the sudden and unexpected loss of weight on his back. Then I saw what had been the weight in his saddle, now a lifeless lump in the dirt under the animal's feet. I started for the door—I'm not quite sure why—to see if he was still alive and could be helped— maybe just a gruesome desire to get a good close look at the body—I don't know, but I never got there. Mose grabbed me by the shoulder and slammed me back against the wall.

"Where you going?" he asked me.

"Maybe he ain't dead," I said.

"He's dead."

"Who was it?" I stammered.

"The law."

"Foster?"

He didn't answer. He was moving quickly about the room, gathering what ammunition he had on hand for the rifle and stuffing it into his jacket pockets. He wrapped up a few pieces of extra clothing along with some food—bread, dried meat and a bag of parched corn—in his old slicker and tied it into a bundle. I was trying to get my head clear.

"Mose, you didn't have to do that," I said.

"I suppose not."

"What are you going to do?"

Mose reached over to pick up the rifle from where he had leaned it against the window ledge and grabbed his bundle in his left hand.

"I'm getting the hell out of here," he said.

"Where'll you go?"

"Up in the hills."

"I'm going with you," I said, and I didn't know why. I just knew that, for some reason, I couldn't let him face what he was going to have to face alone.

"Charlie," he said, "there ain't no reason for you to get messed up in this. You'll be all right here. Go back into town. Tell them they can find their goddamned lawdog out in my yard, and they can find me up in the hills. But if they come looking, some of them gonna stay up there with me."

"I'm going with you, Mose."

"Charlie, what about your momma and daddy—and what about Velma?"

"I'm going."

He leaned back against the wall and looked at me for a bit.

"Okay, Charlie," he finally said. "We'll go by your place on the way up and pick up your rifle, if you're going to be so damn stubborn about it."

We were on our way out the back door when Mose suddenly remembered something, and he quickly crossed the room to his crude, homemade desk and picked up the old, worn copy of Lord Byron's poems that he liked to read so much, stuffed it inside his shirt and once more headed out the door.

We hurried through the woods to my place, which was only a couple of miles, and I gathered up what few necessaries I could quickly lay my hands on—tobacco and papers, coffee, a can to cook it in, and a couple of tin cups. When we left my house, not walking toward town, but out the other direction toward the hills, the two of us together with our rifles in our hands, the whole thing all of a sudden seemed like a bad dream. I felt like we were just going out hunting, the way we had done so many times before—just like this—well, almost like this. Always before when we had gone out this way, to hunt, with our rifles in our hands, there had been three of us. I looked up and around, half expecting to see Henry somewhere nearby, and when he wasn't there, I began to think about that empty saddle back at Mose's house, and both spaces sort of moved in and took over my mind, and I felt empty inside and wondered if anything would ever be the same again.

It had been about the middle of the morning when we left our houses—I don't know the time any closer than that—and we just walked deeper into the woods, farther up into the hills, without saying a word to one another. Mose automatically took the lead, as he always had, and I just naturally followed along. It was well past noon before Mose stopped walking and sat down beneath a tree to rest up and to let me get something to eat. He wouldn't touch any food. I wanted to do like he did—to be like him—but I was too hungry. I ate some dry bread and parched corn in silence. Then Mose got up and I followed, and he led the way to where the creek ran nearby. We drank fresh water from the creek, and, still without a word, he started walking again—still in the same direction. I wanted to ask him how long he thought he would keep walking—how far he thought he would go. I wanted somehow to try to make some sense out of what was happening, but I knew what he would say to me if I opened my mouth about it—that he had told me to keep out of it and that if I was having second thoughts about it now, I could still go back to town and not be involved in any way. So I kept my mouth shut. When Mose finally decided that it was time for us to settle down for a bit and rest, I dug into my bundle of provisions for tobacco and papers, and we rolled us some smokes. Mose always rolled his better than me. We were just sitting there under the trees, waiting for the sun to go down, quietly smoking, when he started to talk.

"Charlie, why'd you come along? I just killed a man."

"I know," I said. "A lawman."

"Yeah, and he was federal," said Mose. "You know what that means? They going to be after me so fast . . ."

"Well, what did you have to go and kill the son of a bitch for, anyhow?" I blurted out, and then I was ashamed I had said anything.

"Aw, hell, Charlie, it don't make no difference. I got nothing left. I got no place to go. They're going to take this place away from us just like they done before, only there ain't no place left for us to move to, I guess. So they're just going to mess up what we got here. I can't fit in."

I was thinking of what Henry might have said.

"Charlie," Mose went on, "you ought to be back in town. Ain't no reason for you to follow me out here on the scout. They going to get me sooner or later, but no one will know you was even with me. And you didn't do nothing, anyway. You go on back home. You'll be all right. You'll fit in okay—you and Velma."

I felt like I should be angry at Mose for what he had just said, but I wasn't. I couldn't be. I was hurt, though, and I felt like I had been somehow left out, and that it wasn't at all fair. I knew what was behind his words when he said that he wouldn't be able to fit in, and I would. I knew what he was really saying. He was saying that I wasn't like him. I wasn't like him and Henry and Malachi, and even if things didn't change, then it would be me that didn't fit in instead of him. He made me feel like a damned puppy dog tagging along at his heels and fetching a stick and having him throw a rock at me and still tagging along. I felt tears welling up in my eyes, and I didn't want him to see them. Damn it, he was a member of a Baptist church, same as me. And who was it had to bring along his goddamned Lord Byron at a time like this? Not me. And if nothing else would prove it, I had come along with him to the hills after he had gone and shot a deputy United States marshal, and I wasn't even sure why he had done it. I somehow sort of took it as Mose's private war, though, and when the chips were down, I had taken his side—joined up with him, so to speak. I was putting my life on the line alongside of him because he was my friend, and I felt like I deserved a little consideration for it. I sure didn't deserve to be insulted and to be put down. Mose must have seen it in my face that I was a little hurt by what he had just said, and he kind of laughed.

"What I'm trying to say, Charlie," he said, "is that there just ain't no place for me in this country no more. I can't be no landowner. It ain't right. I don't want no part of it. But you being raised up in your daddy's store in town—why, you could fit right in with no problems. You see what I mean? There just ain't no reason for you to throw everything away because of what I done."

"Mose, I'm staying."

He shrugged his shoulders, leaned back against the tree he was sitting under, and took a long draw on his cigarette. He didn't say any more. And I started to think back. I started to think about when we were just kids, me and Mose and Henry, and how things were, and to wonder how they got to be the way they turned out.

CHAPTER ONE

For some reason, I'm not quite sure why, I got to thinking about our old schoolteacher, Mr. Franklin, back when Mose and me were going to school together. He's the one who first got Mose interested in Lord Byron. He used to read poems to us a lot in class—just stand up there in front of the classroom and read poems—and it was all I could do to keep from falling asleep. One day I did fall asleep, and the next thing I knew I woke up because Mose was shaking me by the shoulder. I looked up real drowsy-like.

"Charlie," Mose said, "wake up."

I looked around and everybody was being real still and quiet—even Mr. Franklin, who was staring right at me. I was embarrassed as hell, but I just sat up as straight as I was able, and it seemed like an awful long time, but finally Mr. Franklin opened his book and started reading again. I remember when we were walking home after school that day, I asked Mose about it.

"Mose," I said, "why the hell did you do that to me? That was a hell of a thing to do. It embarrassed the shit out of me."

(I always liked to curse a lot when I was around Mose, because I wasn't allowed to at home. And I like to say "ain't" and stuff like that, because at home I was made to speak proper. I guess to this day my language is kind of mixed up because of that.)

"Mr. Franklin made me do it, Charlie," Mose said. "He was just reading poems, you know, and all of a sudden you snored, you goddamn oaf. You snored right out loud—in the middle of a poem."

And then he acted out the scene for me.

" 'When a man hath no freedom . . .'

"*Snort. Honk.*

"Everyone started to giggle, and Mr. Franklin had to stop reading. He told me to reach over and wake you up. Hell, I had to do it, Charlie."

Mose seemed to think that I deserved what I got just a little for having fallen asleep, not just in the classroom, which was bad enough, but during the time when Mr. Franklin was reading poems to us—and not just any poems, but Lord Byron's poems.

It hadn't taken Mr. Franklin long to see that Mose was a pretty serious student, and Lord knows there wasn't many like that among us in those days, or if they were, they were the kind who could just barely write their own names and were going to school so they could learn to read newspapers and public notices like reward posters and things. Me and Mose were just teenagers at that time, but some of the kids in the class were older than Mr. Franklin. Anyhow, Mr. Franklin really liked Mose, because Mose was serious and because he liked Lord Byron. I think Mr. Franklin thought it was astonishing that an Indian, and a full-blood at that, liked English poetry. And there was more than that. There was that day when Mose kept Mr. Franklin from getting his plow cleaned right there in the old classroom.

It was another one of those days when Mr. Franklin was reading poems to us, and it was Lord Byron again. And this white kid named Jerry Smith, who was maybe twenty years old but he'd never learned even to read too well, started to snicker and pop off some, and he got a couple of his friends started in, too. Mr. Franklin called Smith up to his desk in the front of the room and told him to bend over the desk, and he pulled a willow switch out of the desk to whip him with. Smith was just about up to the desk, and he started to back off, looking over his shoulder a little to see what his friends were doing.

"Oh no," he said, "you ain't going to use that goddamned switch on my ass."

"Mr. Smith," said Mr. Franklin, "as a white, and a son of a renter on Cherokee land, you are allowed to attend school here free by the good graces of the Cherokee Nation. You should show a little appreciation for that privilege. Come on."

Smith just stood there.

"Smith," said Mr. Franklin, "am I going to have to drag you up here to whip you?"

And just then Ed Johnson, another *yoneg*, stood up beside Smith, and Smith grinned.

"Yeah, Franklin," he said, "why don't you just by God try that?"

And then two more of the white boys stood up, and Mr. Franklin started to back up, kind of slow and cautious, toward the left-hand corner of the room, back behind his desk where the old potbellied stove stood. When he got close to the stove, and the whites hadn't yet started toward him, he reached back real quick and jerked the iron poker out of the stove and held it in his right hand like a sword.

"Come one, come all," he shouted. "This rock shall fly from its firm base as soon as I."

It sounded crazy, and it slowed them down, but just for a few seconds. Then Ed spoke up.

"Well," he said, "what are we waiting for, huh? Let's take him."

But just as they started to move sort of diagonally across the front of the room, Mose, who had a seat on the front of the left side of the room, stood up real fast and faced them, and without thinking at all about what I might be getting myself into, I stood up right beside him. As it turned out, the Cherokees outnumbered the whites in the school, and since all of us had stood up between Mr. Franklin and the whites, they stopped going at him and just stood there for a couple of seconds. Then they sat back down. Mr. Franklin looked like he was real relieved, and he put the poker back and picked up the switch from where he had let it drop on the floor.

"All right, Smith," he said.

And Smith went up there and took his licking.

Well, we thought that was that, but the next morning when we got to school, we could see right away that Mr. Franklin had got a pretty good going over from somebody. Mose and me both wondered all day long what had happened to him, but we couldn't just up and ask him right there in front of the whole class, so we waited until school was over, and then we just sort of hung around the room when everybody except Mr. Franklin had left.

"Something I can do for you boys?" said Mr. Franklin.

"Aw, no, I guess not, Mr. Franklin," said Mose, and he was just looking at the floor.

I was just looking at Mose, not really knowing why we hadn't gone on out with everybody else.

"Well, then," said Mr. Franklin, "I'll see you in the morning."

He had finished gathering up his books and papers, and he started toward the door.

"Mr. Franklin," said Mose, following him out, "I was wondering,

Mr. Franklin, if you know if there's someplace where I could buy me one of them books. One of them Lord Byron books. So I could read them poems myself."

"One of those books, Moses. Those books."

"Yes, sir, that's what I meant. One of those Lord Byron books."

"I don't think I've seen any around here," said Mr. Franklin, and he was on his way out of the building with Mose and me tagging along. "I guess we're just not civilized enough out here in Indian Territory for the stores to stock up on Lord Byron."

He shut and locked the door to the schoolhouse.

"Well," he said, "I'd better be on my way home."

But he looked for all hell like he really didn't want to leave us. I was beginning to feel awkward. Then Mose took over the situation.

"Mr. Franklin, can me and Charlie walk home with you? It maybe ain't none of our business, but, well, it looks like you might have had some trouble on the way home yesterday, and, well, we just thought you might like some company."

Mr. Franklin looked a little embarrassed, and then he smiled.

"Yes, I would," he said. "Thank you."

On the way to his house, he told us what had happened. Jerry and Eddie and a couple of their friends had jumped him the day before while he was walking home alone and beat up on him some. We all guessed it was to get even for when he had whipped Jerry. And the way they had been acting in school all day, just looking at him funny, he was afraid that they had in mind doing the same thing again. We saw them, all right, but I guess when they saw that he had some company this time and it wouldn't be quite as easy, they changed their minds and decided to go on somewhere else for their fun. After that, Mr. Franklin bought himself a pistol, and he would walk to school with his coat open in front so that you could see that big pistol sticking out the front of his pants, and when he came into the classroom, he would take it out of his pants and place it there on his desk right in front of him. When the day was over, the first thing he would do was pick up his pistol and stick it back in his pants. He didn't have any more trouble after that.

We did, though, walk to his house occasionally with him after school from then on, and we began to feel that he was a little more than just a teacher. He was kind of a good friend. He wasn't a friend the way me and Mose were friends, but, well, we liked him. Mose asked him all kinds of questions about Lord Byron, and sometimes we talked about going hunting. Mose and me had been going out in the hills with Mose's big brother, Henry, since we were just little kids, just as soon as Henry felt like we were big enough to tag along, and Mr. Franklin, being from back east somewhere, seemed kind of interested in hearing about our hunting trips. One day, it was getting along toward the end of Mose's and my last year of school, Mr. Franklin asked us if we thought Henry would mind if we took him along with us one of these times. He said that he liked to hunt deer, and he hadn't been able to do any hunting for quite some time. Ever since he had taken on the job of running our school he had been pretty busy, and besides that, he really didn't know the country very well. Mose agreed right away. We left Mr. Franklin at his house and ran most of the way out of town and into the woods to the log cabin that Mose's father, old Malachi Pathkiller, had built a few years back when he became disgusted with civilization and progress and moved his family away from it. Old Malachi was nowhere to be seen, but Henry was out in back of the cabin with nothing on but a pair of trousers. He was chopping wood. He looked up when he heard us coming.

" 'Siyo, Charlie," he said, "what the hell you doing way out here on a school day? Ain't you scared your daddy'll bust your butt for you?"

"Naw, hell, no, Henry," I said. "He ain't done that for a couple of years now. Hell, I ain't no goddamn kid no more."

Then I started thinking about what my old man might say when I got home late. Of course, I hadn't exactly lied to Henry. He wouldn't have busted my butt. I was too old for that, but he would probably be pretty upset with me, and he would certainly let me know it. He didn't really approve of my spending so much time with Mose, because Mose and his family were full-bloods and they lived outside of town, and they weren't even really farmers. In other words, as my old man would have said, they were lazy, country full-bloods, and it was backwoods Indians like them who were making things rough for the rest of us Cherokees who were really trying to make something out of ourselves and out of our territory. From Daddy's point of view, the only smart thing for a full-blood to do was to marry white, and to get a job in town and try to live like a white man. Then someday, he figured, if things went right, why, you probably wouldn't even know what an Indian was anymore because the races would be so mixed by then that we would all look white, and then there wouldn't be any more problems like the time when they made all our families move out here from back east. And, I don't know, maybe he was right, because our family had done a pretty good job of just that already. Just look at me. But I don't know what was wrong with me that I couldn't feel comfortable with that idea the way Daddy was. I just never did feel like I could be happy in a world without any Indians in it, and I didn't think that I'd even like it if they made our Nation into part of a new state the way they were talking about, but Daddy was all for statehood, and everybody was saying that it was going to happen no matter what. I guess that maybe I'd listened to Henry too much.

Mose brought me out of the conversation that I was having with myself when he spoke to Henry.

"Hey," he said, "we still going hunting Friday?"

"Yup. Any reason I should change my plans?"

"No, I just wanted to check."

"What's the matter? You got something coming up you don't want to go? You ain't got to go if you don't want to."

"No, it ain't that, Henry. Charlie and me are still planning on going. We want to know if we can bring along someone else."

"Who?"

"Mr. Franklin wants to go deer hunting. I told him we'd take him out."

"You what?"

"Well, goddamnit, Henry, if you don't want to do it, you don't have to. Me and Charlie, we'll take him out by ourselves another time. You ain't got to do it."

"Shit. If I was to let you two go out in the woods with guns and that *yoneg* schoolteacher, wouldn't neither one of you be likely to come back. That *gule*'d likely shoot the both of you by mistake. Think you're deers or something. I'll have to watch all three of you. Goddamn."

We figured that was about as cheerful an agreement as we were likely to get out of Henry, so we accepted it and let it go at that. We told Mr. Franklin the next day at school and made all the arrangements. Henry had been out tracking for the last day or so and had found where a good-sized buck slept at night, so we were going to go out on Friday evening and get him as he was coming back to go to sleep. That sounded real good to Mr. Franklin, since he wouldn't have to get up early to go teach on Saturday morning. We decided that on Friday after school, Mose and I would just go on home as usual, but just as soon as I had had my supper, I would hurry on over to Mr. Franklin's house, and then I would take him out to Mose and Henry's place.

CHAPTER TWO

On Friday I did just like we'd planned, and when me and Mr. Franklin were getting close to Mose's place with our rifles and knives and stuff, Mose came trotting through the trees to meet us. He was doing his best to hurry us along without telling Mr. Franklin to get the lead out, so I figured that Henry was getting impatient and had been giving him a hard time. Mr. Franklin just kind of strolled along, looking around at the trees like he was trying to remember where he had gone and watch where he was going. I guess it made sense, as he was somewhere in the woods where he'd never been before, but it made me a little nervous knowing how Henry felt about the whole thing. When we got up to the cabin, we found Henry outside lying on his back in the dirt with his rifle across his chest and his head resting against the stump of a tree that he used for splitting logs on. He had his old hat on so it covered up his face.

"They're here, Henry," said Mose.

Henry didn't move.

"Hey, Henry."

Mose kicked at Henry's feet. Henry slowly lifted up the edge of his hat so that one eye peeked out from under it.

"Oh," he said, "you boys ready to go, are you?"

"Yeah, Henry."

"You real sure, now? I don't want to rush nobody."

"We're ready to go, Henry," said Mose.

Henry got up slowly, using one hand on the stump to help himself. "Well," he said, "if you're goddamn sure you're ready, then let's go." He headed into the woods without another word, and Mose followed him. I didn't think that I should leave Mr. Franklin to take up the rear, so I let him go next and fell in behind. Henry and Mose moved right along just as easy as I move down the sidewalk in town to go from my house to Daddy's store or something. Ordinarily, I don't have much trouble in the woods, especially when I'm with Mose and Henry, and we're going mostly places that I've been maybe a thousand times before with them, but this time it was just a little different, because Mr. Franklin was there between us. He couldn't move along as quickly as they did. Not only did he have to look everywhere he stepped and watch the bushes and low branches to keep them out of his face, but once or twice he got his jacket hung up on something, and then, too, he just didn't have it in him to keep up with them. He was beginning to breathe a little heavy after we'd been walking awhile, and I was real relieved when I saw Henry up ahead stop and raise his hand in a signal for us to hold up. Then he put a finger up to his lips like a sign to shush us, and he started to walk again. Mr. Franklin looked back at me, and I told him in a low whisper that we must be getting close, and that Henry wanted us to keep quiet from here on. We went on for another minute or so before Henry stopped us again. We were on the side of a hill facing down. Between us and the bottom of the hill was a lot of brush, besides all the trees. Henry pointed down the hill to show us where the spot he had found was. We couldn't see it from where we were, but we knew generally where to watch for the appearance of the buck. Then he pointed out a few places where we could kind of settle down to wait and still have a good view of the area. He went down the hill a ways, then Mose went down, not quite as far and off a little to Henry's right. Mr. Franklin and me stayed most of the way up the hill and were right close together. Mr. Franklin settled back against a tree and wiped his forehead with the back of his arm. He looked tired. It was a few minutes before he had caught his breath again, but then he straightened up and seemed more interested in where we were and what was going on again.

Usually, when I had been out with Henry and Mose, we tracked whatever we were hunting for, or just walked and kept our eyes open, but this way of getting a deer was new to me and seemed a little strange. I could see that Mr. Franklin was beginning to get a little impatient just sitting there under a tree and waiting, and I wouldn't have told Mose or Henry for the world, but I felt the same way. I tried to look calm and patient, but I was afraid that I would fall asleep after a while if the damn buck didn't hurry up and come on back home. I felt kind of guilty being that impatient, and then my muscles started to get stiff and sore from just sitting there in the same position, and I got worried that I would have to move and that it would make too much noise. About then Mr. Franklin did move, and it seemed as if you could hear the leaves and bushes rustle all through the woods. At least Henry heard them, because I saw him turn his head toward where we were and give a real hard look. I decided right then that I was going to freeze in that same position if I never was able to move again. I wasn't going to make any noise and cause Henry to think that I couldn't handle myself in the woods, but I was sure glad when that animal finally came along like Henry had said he would.

I think that Henry was the first one of us to see the buck. At least, I know he saw him before I did or before Mr. Franklin did, because from where I was I noticed first a very slight reaction from Henry, like he just stretched his neck a little more or something, so I looked in the direction he was looking, and then I saw it. At just about the same instant, out of the corner of my eye, I could see Mose look around toward Mr. Franklin to see if he had spotted it or not. We had all agreed beforehand to let him get off the first shot, but Mose and Henry weren't out just for fun, and they weren't about to let that buck get away. I reached over, quick but easy, and touched Mr. Franklin on the arm, and he looked up and saw it. Then his rifle went up, and he held it there for only a second before he snapped off a shot. The buck gave a little jerk, like he wanted to leap forward, but he didn't go anyplace. Mr. Franklin had hit him in the hindquarters, and the shot must have paralyzed his back legs or something, at least momentarily. Henry stood straight up from where he'd been hiding, and as he was standing, he shouted.

"Damn," he said, as he squeezed the trigger.

The buck dropped, and Henry hurried on down to where it had fallen. Mose jumped up and ran after him. I followed with Mr. Franklin right behind me. I could see that Mose was busy telling Henry something, but he was talking in Cherokee, so even if I had been able to hear, I couldn't have understood what he was saying. When he stopped, I heard Henry mutter to himself.

"*Yoneg,*" he said.

Well, I knew that word. "White," it means. I figured that Mose had told him to take it easy on Mr. Franklin, because he was not only a friend, but he was our teacher, for Chrissake. Henry knelt beside the buck and said something in Cherokee in a low voice. I didn't know the words, but I knew that he must be apologizing to the spirit of the dead animal. He always did that, and maybe this time he felt like he had even more reason for it. I don't know. When Mr. Franklin got on down to the foot of the hill, Mose stepped over to meet him.

"Well," he said, "you got a pretty nice one there, Mr. Franklin."

"Yes," said Mr. Franklin, "he's a real beauty."

Henry reached out with his knife and slit the animal's throat. I helped Henry and Mose hang it up to a nearby tree, and then I just stood back out of the way with Mr. Franklin and watched them as they set to work dressing it out.

"Henry," said Mr. Franklin, "I'm sorry if I spoiled the hunt for you. The boys said it would be all right, and I guess you only put up with me because of them, but thanks for letting me come along. I really enjoyed it."

Henry didn't look around from what he was doing, but I guess Mr. Franklin's apology must have caught him off guard.

"Aw, hell," he said, "that's all right. I . . ."

The rest of what he said just trailed off into some muttering that I couldn't hear. Then he raised his voice again.

"Charlie," he said, "why don't you two start a fire and put on the coffee?"

We started to do that.

"Hey, teacher," said Henry.

We all turned around to look at him just as he raised up a bloody hand holding the heart of the deer. It went dripping up to his mouth, and he took a bite. Then he offered it to Mr. Franklin, who just sat there astonished.

"Well, come on, teacher. You put a bullet into him, too. Have some."

"No. I, uh, no, thanks."

"Come on."

"Henry," said Mose, *"hlesdi."*

Henry shrugged and turned to me.

"Charlie?" he said, offering the bloody heart.

I took it from Henry and had my bite, then gave it to Mose. Mr. Franklin had taken advantage of this seeming change of focus and was busying himself with the coffeepot. None of us said much of anything after that for a while. We just waited for the pot to boil, and even though I felt a little sorry for Mr. Franklin for the way Henry was treating him—maybe not sorry, maybe just uncomfortable—I felt like I could understand why Henry was doing it. We had ignored almost all the ritual that usually accompanied our hunts. To begin with, we had been late, and then, well, Mr. Franklin just didn't fit in. He didn't understand, and he probably never could. At any rate, Henry didn't feel like teaching him and looked upon his being along with us as an intrusion and a disruption of the patterns and rhythms of the hunt.

When our coffee was made, and we all had cups in our hands, Mr. Franklin, after a short period of embarrassed silence, reached inside his jacket.

"Mose," he said, "I brought along something for you, kind of in exchange for your setting this whole thing up for me."

He brought out an old book which Mose and me both recognized right away and stretched out his arm to hand it to Mose.

"School year's about over, and I know most of the poems," he said. "Anyway, I think I can find me another copy without too much trouble."

Mose took the book and just held it with both hands up in front of his face for a while before he could say anything. He looked to me like he was afraid it might break or he might get it dirty or something.

"Thanks," he said finally. "Thank you, Mr. Franklin."

Henry muttered something to himself and rolled over to play with the fire. Mose was just staring at that damn book. I poured myself another cup of coffee.

"Speaking of the end of school," said Mr. Franklin, "what are you two boys planning to do with yourselves now?"

"Oh," I said, "I just start working full-time in Daddy's store. I been working all along after school and on Saturdays and in the summer. It won't really be much different, I guess, except that I'll be doing it all the time now and not going to school. Daddy says that one of these days the store'll be all mine, and so I've got to learn how to handle all the different angles of running it and everything. I guess it's not too exciting."

"There are lots worse things for a man to do with his life, Charlie," said Mr. Franklin. "In a few years, when you start thinking about becoming a family man, you'll be real glad your daddy built up that store for you to move into."

"Yeah," I said, "I guess so," but I didn't really believe it.

"What about you, Mose?"

"Well, I had a talk with Mr. Lawson. You know, the blacksmith. And he said that he'd put me to work and learn me the trade. That's about all, I guess. I just want to get me a good job and earn a decent living."

He paused for a few seconds before he went on.

"Have a trade," he said. "Because, uh, besides all that, I'm fixing to take me a wife."

"What?" I said.

"I was going to tell you, Charlie. It just hadn't come up yet, that's all."

I was real surprised, but I guess I shouldn't have been. Way back in the woods and up in the hills, at just about the farthest point back in the hills that I had ever been with Mose and Henry when we went hunting, was a family of full-bloods named Beaver, who lived in a small log cabin. There was the old man and woman and their two daughters, Sarah and Annie. I guess that Henry had met them all sometime before he had started to take me and Mose out with him, but we had all known them for several years by this time. I never really knew the old people because they didn't speak any English, and neither one of the girls spoke it well, but I could talk to them. Me and Mose had just been kids when we met them, but even so it didn't take us very long to figure out that Henry and Sarah were carrying on with each other out there. Sometimes he would set us to cleaning the squirrels or rabbits or whatever we had shot, or if we hadn't shot anything yet, he would send us off by ourselves to see what we could do on our own, and he would slip off somewhere with Sarah. Anyhow, Sarah's little sister, Annie, was about two years younger than Mose, and they had gotten to be very close the last few years, so even though I was surprised at his announcement, I knew that Annie was the girl. And we were finishing school and were the right age to start thinking about marriage, I guessed. I had started seeing a girl now and then myself just recently. Her name was Velma.

Anyhow, Mr. Franklin heard all of Mose's plans for the future, and he looked thoughtful for a bit before he spoke again.

"I think that's real fine, Mose," he said. "You can do a lot for your people, I believe. All they, I mean you, all of you, all you really need is someone with the guts to do it—to show the rest that it can be done. And you just may be the one to show them, Mose, to show them that they can all be a part of civilization and not just its victims."

Henry had been quiet all this time, but that last was more than he could sit still for.

"Bullshit," he said, turning on Mr. Franklin. "You think we ain't civilized? Don't know nothing about civilization? You think we're all a bunch of ignorant savages out here?"

"No, Henry, I didn't say that."

"Let me tell you about civilization. We had one a long time ago. A good one. It worked for us. Then the white man come along. He wanted land. He took land. When we didn't have very much left, he wanted it all. Some Cherokees thought that the white man didn't want savages for neighbors. That's why they were trying to get us out of there. So we made our civilization over to match yours, with churches and schools and all that shit. Papa—my papa and Mose's papa—he was a lawmaker in the Cherokee Nation. He could read and write in two languages. Can you read Cherokee, teacher? Can you even talk it? We can talk your language, maybe not as pretty as you'd like it, but we can talk it.

"And my papa, he was a politician. And him and them other Cherokee politicians, they built a Nation in the east. It had everything yours has got. Voting districts. Popular elections. A written constitution. A police force. Yes, sir. We was acting just like white folks, so that we'd make good neighbors for them redneck Georgia crackers. We even found gold and commenced to mine it. The trouble was, the more we done, the more attractive we made our land to your people, so they moved us out here. They said they'd leave us alone out here—forever. Do you know, teacher, that there's more white folks than Indians in the Cherokee Nation already? And they're talking about making it a state? We come out here and rebuilt, and the same damn thing's happening again. We done too good a job. We built it up the way whites like it, so they're going to take it away from us."

Henry paused to catch his breath. It was the most talk I can ever remember coming out of him at one time. Mr. Franklin tried to answer, but he was too slow on the draw.

"We built the whole damn thing," said Henry. "Twice. Don't tell me about civilization. That town you live in and that schoolhouse you teach in, they were built by Cherokees, not by white men. We should have stayed the way we was to begin with. There wouldn't have been as much to steal from us, and it was a better way of life, anyhow."

"But you're wrong, Henry," said Mr. Franklin. "Can't you see that? I don't deny there's been wrong done—on both sides. But you've got to face facts, man. The United States government is here to stay, and you've got to become a part of civilization, Henry, you and Mose and all of your people. You've got to move with progress, or it will roll right over you."

Henry pitched what was left of his coffee out into the darkness away from our fire. He stood up and picked up his rifle.

"Look," he said to me and Mose, ignoring Mr. Franklin, "you two can manage everything from here, can't you? I'm sorry, Mose, I done my best, but, well, he's just full of shit."

Then he disappeared into the trees.

The rest of that year went by fast, and Mose started learning to be a blacksmith and saving his money. He married Annie all right, and it didn't take much for them to live the way they wanted to. He went down the creek from where his old man lived, and he built him his own little cabin. He planted a garden, and between the job and the garden and the hunting he did, they were doing very well. We used to talk about how much fun it would be when I finally decided to settle down and marry Velma, and we'd build me a cabin out there so that we'd be neighbors, and our kids would grow up together out in the woods. Things went on like that for about a year, and then Annie died trying to have a baby. Mose carried both of them up the hill a ways from their cabin and buried them himself in the old Cherokee way, with a little house built over the grave, and then he went off up into the hills. He didn't come back for a whole week, and some folks were wondering if he'd ever come back, but I was pretty sure that he would.

I had been working all this time as a clerk in my daddy's store, and one morning, I guess it was about the third or fourth morning that Mose was gone, I was sitting at the breakfast table with my folks finishing my coffee, when all of a sudden and for no reason, Daddy started in.

"I hear from old Lawson," he said, "that Mose Pathkiller's been gone from work for several days now."

I looked up from my coffee, but he wasn't looking at me. He had his face all the way into his scrambled eggs and his gravy and both arms going at it, so I didn't bother replying to what he had said. I had been thinking about one more cup of coffee before going to open up the store, but all of a sudden all I wanted was to get out of the house, because I could kind of sense what was about to happen. But I didn't make it. I was almost to the door when Daddy, still with both arms going, stopped me.

"I always told you that boy would come to no good," he said. "Knew he wouldn't be able to hold on to that job much longer."

And he was so damned proud of himself for having been proved right, as he saw it. I wanted to smash something. I wanted to shove his face into his plate. But I didn't.

"Daddy," I said, "his wife just died."

"Well, the world's got to go on. A job's a job. It's too bad about that girl, but Lawson's got a shop to run. Backwoods Indians can't seem to understand that. It's economics, Charlie. Economics. We got to take things in stride and keep going."

"You don't understand," I said, but he didn't hear me, I guess.

"I just don't think he'd ever have amounted to much anyhow," he said.

I blew up. I shouldn't have done it, I know, but I just seemed to lose control. I was yelling before I knew what I was doing.

"Damn it," I said. "Mose is my best friend. He loved Annie, and she's dead. Ain't you got no feelings? And she was having a baby, and Mose was so happy looking forward to it, and then they both of them died, and . . . Aw, what the hell."

Mama had kept quiet all this time, but what I said was too much for her.

"Charles," she said. "Don't you raise your voice to your father. And don't you use that kind of language in my house. I won't stand for it. We raised you better than that, Charles."

I knew that if I opened my mouth again, what would come out would only be that much worse than what I had already said, so I just jerked the door open and left for the store in a big hurry. I opened up the store, and Daddy didn't show up until some time later. I guessed that he and Mama were talking about me and wondering where they had gone wrong or something like that. When he did show up, he didn't say anything more about our fight, so I didn't either. He must have figured that Mama had told me off well enough, and he'd just let it drop. I was quiet and on my best behavior the rest of the day, but it was kind of uncomfortable around the store unless we was busy with customers. Around supper time, he said that he was going home and for me to lock up for him. I said okay and asked him to remind Mama that I wouldn't be home for supper because I had been invited over to eat with Velma and her folks. He said he would and left me alone to lock up.

CHAPTER THREE

Supper with Velma's folks didn't turn out to be much help to me in the mood I was in. I kept thinking about what had happened at home that morning, and I couldn't help but think how much like my folks hers were. It seemed like we would never get finished with the damn meal, and all I could do was wish that Mose was back and the two of us could be out somewhere in the woods, away from all this. I wondered where he was and what he was doing, and I kept feeling very stiff and awkward, like at any time I would spill coffee or drop some potatoes in my lap or something. I did manage to get through the meal, though, without any such awful thing happening; and then, after a few very quiet minutes with some simple-minded attempts at polite conversation between me and Velma's folks, Velma managed to get us out of trouble by suggesting that, as it was such a nice night out, she and I should go out for a short walk around the town. Her mother gave her a knowing look with a kind of warning mixed in with it, and said for us to be nice and have fun and not be gone too long. I promised to take good care of her, and we got the hell out of there and walked straight out to the edge of town and a little ways on to the graveyard, where we always went to make love.

Velma and I had been seeing a lot of each other for some time, and everyone had begun to assume that we were going to be married one of these days, and before we knew it, the two of us had assumed it too, without ever having really talked about it. I had never even asked her or anything, but I discovered that sometime or other we had both started talking about when we would be married. Our families both approved of the idea, because both families were very much alike. Velma had a little Cherokee blood in her, I'm not sure how much, but the point is that both of us came from families that called themselves Cherokee, and both families had been mixed-blood families for so long that nobody could even remember a full-blood ancestor. Both families called the full-bloods out in the hills backwards Indians, and both families were looking forward to becoming private landowners in a brand-new state. Of course, that also meant that both families were looking forward to the total destruction of the Cherokee Nation.

Anyway, me and Velma had been going to the graveyard pretty often for a while by this time, and it was beginning to keep us both pretty nervous. We kept thinking that maybe she would get pregnant, and every time her time of the month came around so that she knew that everything was okay, she would find some excuse to come down to the store to buy some little something, but really just so she could see me to let me know. She would go over to some counter in the store where there weren't any customers nearby and start to look at something and act like she needed some help from me. Then I would go over there as soon as I got the chance, and she would say something like "It started today" in a real low voice, and every time I would take a deep breath and let out a long sigh and then make a very appropriate and witty comment. Usually something like "Good." Then the very next week or so, first chance we got, we would go out to the graveyard again and start to go through the whole damn miserable cycle for another month.

Needless to say, after this had gone on for some time, it got to be just a little too much to take, so we had finally and formally decided to go ahead and get married. I had told Mose (this had been just a little while before Annie had died), and, like I said before, he had helped me to put up a nice little cabin not too far from where his was out in the woods. Everything was fine between the two families, and between me and Velma, except none of them could figure out why I wanted to take her out there to live, and they kept at me about putting up a neat little frame house in town. Finally, I quieted them down some by saying that since I had already put up the cabin, there was no reason me and Velma couldn't go out there to live for a while after we got married, and that I would start building a real home in town as soon as I could afford to. Besides, I told them, people like to be off by themselves right after they get married, sort of like a honeymoon. They accepted that, or, at least, seemed to. Of course, they had no way of knowing that the graveyard had been sufficient for us for some time, so my reason of privacy was really just an excuse to shut them up with. Anyway, they probably thought that after we were married, Velma would be miserable out there in the woods and would nag me into moving back into town.

There was to be a dance on Saturday night following that evening I had supper with Velma and her folks. It was to be held downtown in the yard of our National Capitol Building. Velma and I had made plans to attend while we were walking from supper to the graveyard.

When Saturday finally rolled around, and I started to think about going to the dance with Velma, and mostly about slipping away from the dance and everybody there to take her back out to the graveyard again, I remembered that Mose was still out in the hills by himself because of Annie and his baby. I didn't at all feel like going after I had remembered all that, but it didn't seem to me that there would be any even halfway graceful way out of it, so I decided that I would just go ahead. I really felt guilty about it, though. I felt like I should still be in mourning or something—certainly not like I should be going out to have a good time. I thought that maybe I just wouldn't suggest the graveyard—that we'd stay at the dance the whole time, and I'd deprive myself in that way, and then I wouldn't feel quite as bad about the whole thing. But the more I thought about that, the less it seemed likely that things would turn out that way. If I managed to keep myself from making the suggestion, Velma would most probably make it herself, and then, on top of that, she would most likely start to pester me to try to find out what was wrong.

Saturday night, just about sundown, I walked over to the Hotchkiss house to pick up Velma. On the way walking to the old Council House, I saw what a stupid thing it had been on my part to think that I would try to hold out, because I made the suggestion to her that we could walk down through the graveyard before going to the dance.

"Why don't we go on to the dance, Charlie, honey," she said, "and then leave just a bit early? We could do it after the dance just as well as before."

"We could go on down there now for a while, and then go on to the dance—and then go back to the graveyard," I said.

She laughed her little laugh that had a sound of superiority in it with a little tolerance for me. Her eyes were sparkling with what looked to me like a love of wickedness.

"But that would be wretched excess, Charlie, honey," she said, and she started to walk much faster.

I hurried along beside her until we got to the dance, and I danced one or two dances with her and one or two with Molly Allen, and I was hating myself the whole time.

After those first few dances, I just dropped out of the way right close to the table where they had the punch, which I had seen Eddie Johnson spike earlier with some bootleg whiskey, and I started to drink about as much as I could manage without calling too much attention to myself. Once I noticed that Velma was dancing with that goddamned Jerry Smith, and then I realized that I really couldn't tell the difference in the way she was having fun with him and the way she did with me, and I noticed how white they both looked and thought that that must be the way I looked with Velma. Then I started thinking about Mose and Annie, and I was so envious I began to wish that Velma was dead and that I was up in the hills.

I don't know how long things went on like that, but finally Velma came on over to where I was standing not far from the punch table, leaning against the trunk of a tree and feeling more than a little woozy. She kind of sidled up to me.

"You've been keeping to yourself tonight," she said.

I just sort of muttered.

"Why, Charlie, honey, I do believe you're just a wee bit tipsy."

"I'm all right," I said.

"Let's go for a little walk, honey, okay?"

"It's about goddamn time," I said, and my tongue felt thick.

We started to ease away from the crowd and stroll down the street, casually, like we were just going for a walk around town. We got a ways away from the dance and everybody there, and neither one of us had said anything further, when we slipped around a corner to get off the main street and started toward the graveyard.

"Charlie," she said, "what's the matter with you tonight? You sure don't seem to be having a good time, and that's not very flattering to me."

I thought about Mose and I thought about Annie, and then I thought about that son of a bitch Jerry.

"There's nothing wrong, Velma," I lied.

"Well, Charlie, you just aren't acting like yourself, and I'm sure that there's something wrong with you. I just hope it doesn't have anything to do with me. I mean, I haven't done anything wrong, have I?"

"Oh no, Velma," I said. "No, you haven't done anything."

And she hadn't, of course. I wasn't mad at her for dancing with Jerry —not really. And it wasn't that I was getting to the point where I didn't like Velma anymore. It wasn't that. It was more like I didn't like what she was, and maybe I didn't like what I was.

"I do wish you'd tell me when something's wrong, Charlie, but if you just don't want to, well, I'm certainly not going to beg you to tell me."

By this time we were walking in the graveyard, and we had come to where Velma's Grandma Hotchkiss was laid to rest, as they say. That was one of her very favorite spots for what we were about to do. We stopped.

"Anyway," she said, "if you don't want to talk about it, why then, I'll just make you forget all about it, and everything will be all right."

She sat down right on top of Grandma Hotchkiss and stretched out along the grave, with her head right at the marker and on some old flowers that had been left there to decorate the grave. Maybe she had put them there herself. And she held her arms out to me, and I lay down beside her. Pretty soon, we got rid of some extra stuff that was in our way, like her bloomers and my trousers, and we started to make love. I almost had to laugh out loud when I thought of how I was not only on top of Velma but on top of old Grandma Hotchkiss, too, but I kept myself from laughing, because I knew I wouldn't be able to tell her what it was that was so funny. We had been there before in that very same position, I don't know how many times, and I don't know why it struck me so funny on that particular occasion. Anyway, something else happened just then that caused me another problem that at the time wasn't at all funny and made me curse myself for having drunk so much at the dance. Velma was never very easily satisfied, and with a disadvantage like I all of a sudden had, I never had a chance. I finally had to just give up trying, and I was embarrassed. I remember thinking that the whole episode was a terrible blow to my manhood, and I really wanted her to understand and to tell me that it was all right because there would always be a next time, but she was pretty disgusted, and she didn't even try to hide the fact from me.

We pulled ourselves together and started home without saying a word to each other. We were probably both of us thinking what a hell of a lot the whole evening left to be desired when, just as we were getting out of the graveyard, we heard this loud yell.

"Wooiiee. Hey, Eddie, looka here what's coming out of the old graveyard."

"Oh, God, Charlie, it's Jerry Smith."

I looked up and saw Jerry Smith and Eddie Johnson standing over by some trees and laughing.

"It's okay," I said. "I'll take care of this."

I was thinking how it was anything but okay, but I took a couple of steps toward Jerry and Eddie.

"Hey, fellows," I said. "Look. Leave us alone and don't say anything about this, okay?"

"Jerry," Eddie said, not paying any attention to me, but staring straight at Velma, "you reckon he's been getting any of that down in the old graveyard?"

"What else would they be doing here this time of night?"

"You guys have got this all wrong," I said. "We're just out for a walk. We had some things to talk over, you know?"

They just grinned and looked at Velma. Jerry took a bottle out of his pocket and drank from it. Eddie leaned back against a tree and rubbed his crotch.

"Hey," I said, trying to appear relaxed and friendly, "just forget all about this, okay?"

"Well," said Eddie, "I don't know about old Jerry here, but I think old Velma might be able to persuade me to keep quiet. What about it, Jer? You think we might be able to make some kind of deal?"

"I might be able to give it some thought. Only thing, she ain't no lady, like you said. She's just another one of them uppity breeds, just like her boyfriend there."

"Wait a minute," I said. "You're talking crazy."

"You think she'll still be uppity after you and me takes turns on her?" said Eddie.

"Look," I said, my voice beginning to tremble, "she's not that kind of girl. Me and Velma, well, we're fixing to get married."

Still they ignored me, and Jerry started to walk past me toward Velma.

"What about it, Miss Velma Hotchkiss?" he said. "You be nice to me and Eddie here, and we won't tell nobody that we seen you coming out of the graveyard with old Charlie and your skirts rumpled up."

I grabbed him by the shoulder and spun him around toward me.

"Now you get the hell out of here," I yelled.

He drove his fist into my stomach, and while I was sinking down to the ground, feeling awful sick, he shouted to Eddie.

"Grab her," he said.

I was trying hard to catch my breath, and I looked up just in time to see Eddie grab hold of Velma's blouse. She screamed out my name. It took just about all the strength I had, but I made a powerful lunge and tackled Eddie around the middle. As the two of us crashed into the dirt, I shouted to Velma.

"Run, Velma," I said. "Get home. Run."

I guess that she did, because all I remember after that was Eddie and Jerry both all over me, and all I could do was to try to keep my hands over my face. They must have finally gotten tired of beating on me, because when they quit I was still conscious, but wishing to God that I wasn't. They left me lying there and went away laughing, apparently just as much satisfied with what they had done to me as they would have been with what they'd have done to Velma. I puked for a while, and then I remembered how disgusted Velma had been with my feeble performance just a little while ago, and it seemed to me that maybe I should've let those two alone with her after all, and everybody'd have been much happier. It would all have been very funny if it hadn't hurt so much.

CHAPTER FOUR

I woke up Sunday morning feeling worse than I could ever remember having felt before in my whole life. I seldom got drunk, and I had never had a beating like that before, and added to all that was the terrible humiliation of the graveyard business. I was awfully glad that it was Sunday and that I didn't have to think about putting in a full day at the store feeling the way I did. I was thinking how nice it would be just to be able to lie in bed and suffer quietly, but I figured that the hassle I'd have with the folks about my not going to church just wouldn't be worth it, so I got painfully out of bed and got myself ready to go. I wasn't looking forward to going to the breakfast table looking the way I did and having to try to explain it to Mama and Daddy, but I thought up what I imagined would be as good an explanation as any, and I went on in to face up to it.

Mama almost dropped the coffeepot when I walked into the kitchen. "Charles," she said. "What on earth has happened to you?"

Daddy just looked up at me when he heard what she said and waited for my explanation.

"Oh, don't worry, Mama," I said. "I'm okay. It looks a lot worse than it feels."

That last part was a very big lie.

"But what have you gotten into?" she asked.

"Oh, last night, on the way home from Velma's house, I met these two guys who wanted to have a little fun, I guess. That's all. It just didn't turn out to be quite as much fun for me."

I thought that it would be best to keep all names out of it and to keep Velma completely out of the whole thing. If my old man had known who it was who had beat me up, he would probably have gone to the law with their names or something. Then, to get even, they would most likely have felt obligated to tell the whole story. And I couldn't very well give the whole reason for the fight, as that would have involved Velma and what we had been doing in the graveyard in the first place. I just hoped that she had had the good sense to keep completely quiet about it at home, and that when she saw me at church she would act like she didn't have any idea what had happened to me or when it had happened.

"Who were they, son?" said Daddy.

"Just a couple of guys. They'd had a little too much to drink at the dance, I guess. Somebody spiked the punch. I don't think they even knew who I was. They probably don't even remember anything about it this morning."

"Well, you're not just going to let them get away with a thing like this, are you? Was it some of those full-bloods?"

I ground my teeth before I could answer that last question.

"No, Daddy," I said. "They were white. And I think it's best to just let the whole thing drop, okay?"

Of course it wasn't okay, but there was really nothing he could do about it, so that was that. We finished breakfast and got ourselves the rest of the way ready to go to church, then left the house to walk there together as we had done every Sunday morning for as far back as I could remember. As we met a few friends along the way and then in front of the church and on the way in, I had to endure the questions and wisecracks about my appearance that one always has to contend with after a fight that has left its marks. The Baptist church that we went to was only a few blocks down one of the main streets in town from our house. There was another one out in the woods a few miles from town that the full-bloods attended, but Mama and Daddy always said that it was just a poor country church and that its preacher was an illiterate full-blood Indian and not a real preacher and, worst of all, those full-bloods practiced heathen conjuring right out behind the church. I had tried to get them to let me go to it once with Mose, but it caused such a noise in the house that you wouldn't believe, so I went to the church in town.

We got to the church a few minutes early. Daddy always made a practice of that, because it gave him a chance to stand around in the churchyard and talk to his friends before the service. Mama usually went on inside. She didn't think it was very becoming for a lady to be seen standing around jawing outside with a bunch of men—especially outside the church. I usually waited outside with Daddy until the Hotchkiss family showed up, and then I would join Velma and go inside.

This morning was no different from any other Sunday morning, except for the way I looked and felt, and when I saw Velma and them coming down the street, I excused myself from Daddy and his friends and went to meet them. I was in a little more of a hurry than usual, because if Velma had been fool enough to tell her folks anything about the fight and the story was any different from the one I had given at home, I didn't want the discovery to be made in front of my old man. When I got close enough for them to get a good look at me, Velma just kind of stopped in her tracks for a second and took both of her hands up to her face like she was startled or something.

"Why, Charlie," she said. "Charlie, whatever happened to you?"

I was so relieved that I gave her a real big smile, and I answered loud enough for her folks to hear too.

"Aw, it's nothing much, Velma," I said.

Then I gave them the whole story—the same one that I had made up that morning and told to my folks. Then Velma's old man started the same kind of stuff as mine had, about how I shouldn't let them get away with it, and I answered him the same way I had answered before, but this time I had some help. Velma had as much to lose from all this as I did—more, since she was a girl.

"I think he's right, Daddy," she said. "Those poor boys were probably so drunk they didn't know what they were doing, and I'm very proud of my Charlie for being such a good Christian and so forgiving. It's really wonderful of you, Charlie. And what a fine thing for us to take with us as we go to church this morning."

After that, there wasn't much that those good Christians could say, so they left well enough alone, and we all went on into the church house. Velma and I could hardly wait for the service to end, we had so much to talk about. Both of us were nervous and fidgety throughout the whole business and had a hard time restraining ourselves, but we managed to last through it without too much wear on our nervous systems. When we were finally let out, we did our best not to look like we were in a big hurry to get out of there. We nodded to everyone, and we had to stop and explain my appearance to a few people. We did eventually make it out through the church door to the outside, though, and then I spoke up.

"Velma, can I walk you home?"

"Why, thank you, Charlie," she said. "I'd be proud."

I offered her my arm rather stiffly. She took it with a great deal of ease and poise, and we started on our way. As soon as we were out of earshot of anyone else, we both started to talk at the same time.

"You go ahead," I said.

"Charlie, I'm so glad that you had the foresight to make up that story. I was so worried about it that I was sick. I was just sick. I didn't sleep a wink all night."

"Yeah, well, I was afraid that you'd say something about it and spoil the whole thing. It was very smart of you to keep quiet and then to put on that act the way you did. Did you get home all right? I wasn't in any shape to find out until quite a while later."

"Oh, I made it home all right, I suppose. If you mean did I get home all in one piece without being caught by those two hooligans and being raped. But I never ran so hard in my whole entire life, and I was so scared I thought I would die right there in the street. Oh, Charlie, it was so awful."

"I'm just glad that it turned out as well as it did, that you got home safe, and that nobody found out about how it all really came about."

"But, Charlie, what if those two awful boys go ahead and tell on us?"

"I don't think they'll do that."

"But they might do it just for pure meanness. I wouldn't put it past either one of them, especially that no-good Jerry Smith."

I wanted to say something about how she had sure changed her opinion of Jerry Smith since early last evening when she had been having such a good time with him at the dance, at least from the way it looked to me, but I didn't.

"They most likely won't ever say anything to anybody, Velma," I said, "because then they'd have to let it out that they're the ones who whipped me so bad, and then people'd start asking why. They couldn't very well let anyone know what they were trying to do, now could they?"

"I guess you're right, Charlie. I certainly hope so. I just don't know what I'd do if it ever got out that—well, what we've been doing out there. Why, my daddy'd likely beat me within an inch of my life."

"I'm really sorry all that had to happen, Velma. I guess even besides all that part of it, I just wasn't much good for anything last night. I guess I sort of ruined your whole evening, and I'm really sorry. I know how you were looking forward to the dance and all, but I was, well, I was thinking about Mose and what he's been going through, and you know how I feel about Mose. I mean, he's the best friend I ever had, and I just couldn't get it all out of my mind."

"Well, I never knew that anybody meant more to you than I do, Charlie. If that's the way you feel about me, I'm just surprised that you didn't let those two have me to do with what they wanted while you went out in the woods to look for your wild friend."

I almost told her that the thought had entered my mind, and now that she mentioned it, I was damned if I knew why I hadn't.

"That's not what I meant, Velma. You know goddamned well that's not what I meant. Who do you suppose I was thinking about when I tried to take on those two bastards all by myself, anyhow? And it looks like what I get for all my concern is first I get the hell knocked out of me and then you start in on me."

"Oh, Charlie." She squeezed my arm closer to her with her own. "Charlie, I'm truly sorry. I know you love me best, and you were wonderful last night with those two, and then this morning too, the way you covered it all up. And you poor dear, you must have had an awful beating, and you did it just for me. Here I've been going on about what a dreadful time I've been having, and I just forgot all about what you went through. Charlie, was it just awful?"

Something in her voice made me think that she was hoping that the answer was going to be yes, and I didn't want her to have that satisfaction.

"No," I said, "it really wasn't nearly as bad as it could have been. It just looks pretty messy, but the truth is that I was so drunk that just a little bit after you got away, I passed out, before they had a chance to hurt me too much."

The lie felt good, and I had been telling lies all morning, so it came easy.

"You're just trying to make it easier on me, I know," she said. "I know that it was awful because your face is so ugly this morning."

Then we both laughed a little, and by this time we were practically in her front yard, so I walked her on up to the door and said good-bye and left for home.

CHAPTER FIVE

After dinner, I walked out to my cabin. I just stood in front of it looking for a few minutes, then I went up to the door, which was not yet hung but was just leaning there in place, and I lifted it out of my way and went on into the house. I sat down on the old tree stump that Mose had carried in to use for a kind of workbench and thought about the last time I had seen Mose. I had gone out to the cabin after a Sunday dinner. Mose and I had been meeting after church on Sundays to work on the place, and even though it was to be my home, he would nearly always be there before me, not just waiting for me to show up, but working away at something. But that Sunday I wasn't really expecting him to show up at all, because I knew the condition that Annie was in, and I had told him not to bother with me, but that, if everything was all right and he got the time, he might come over for just long enough to let me know if he was the daddy of a little boy or a little girl, or, as Henry used to say, a ballsticks or a sifter. I didn't want to go over to his cabin, because I was afraid that I might show up at a bad time or something. Anyway, he just grinned real big.

"You'll know, Charlie," he said. "I'll see to that."

Then he took the door from out of the door frame where he had been trying its fit and leaned it against the wall.

"That's ready for hanging now," he said.

"Later," I said. "Right now, I want you to go back home to Annie, and I'm going to call on Velma."

As things turned out, it was quite some time before I got back to that damned door. Like I've been trying to say, that Sunday I'd gone out there thinking that Mose probably wouldn't show up for a while, and when he did show up, he'd only have a minute or so to give me the big news, and I was going to try to hang up that door by myself. So I was just a little startled when I got there and picked the door out of my way so I could get in, and there sat Mose inside all by himself and not doing a damned thing but staring at the wall.

"Mose?"

He didn't answer me. He just stared straight ahead.

"Mose?"

I knew what I wanted to ask, what I would have to ask if he didn't just go ahead and tell me. There was something about the way he was just sitting there, and there was the fact that if things were okay, he shouldn't even have been there at all. Still, I couldn't bring myself to ask it.

"Mose? How long you been here?"

"Since about sunup."

He still hadn't looked at me.

"But, Mose, everything's all right, ain't it? I mean"—and I nearly choked on the next word, but I had to go ahead and get it said. "Annie —and the baby—they . . ."

"They dead, Charlie."

I could hardly breathe, and I felt like I might pass out any second, but I had to try to keep ahold of myself because Mose sure had problems enough without having to worry about me. I leaned back against what I thought was going to be the wall but turned out to be the loose door. It started to slide with my weight, and it was all I could do to keep from falling on my ass. I thought, what a hell of a time to get clumsy, Charlie. What a hell of a stupid goddamn time. Mose was still just sitting and staring, and I felt more useless than I'd ever felt before. I wanted to go ahead and cry to show him I cared, to let him know he wasn't alone in his grief, and then I wanted to go over to him and take him in my arms and just put his head on my shoulder and let him cry until all the misery and all the heartaches were gone. I just stood there.

"Can I, uh, can I help you with anything, Mose?"

The only thing in the world I could think of that he might need any help with was grave digging, and after I'd asked the question I hated myself for it.

"No, thanks, Charlie," he said. "Everything's done. I done it first thing this morning."

Then he had gotten up and walked out of the cabin without another word, and I had let him. As I watched him walk into the woods, I remembered how he had promised that I would know, and I knew that he had been waiting there in the dark of my unfinished cabin just to keep that promise. Then I realized that I couldn't remember the details of the full-blood funeral practices, and I didn't know, if Mose had buried them that morning, if that meant that they had died last night or four days ago. I didn't know, and I felt stupid. Anyway, that had been the last time I saw Mose before he went off into the hills by himself and old Lawson had commenced to complain about him missing work. And there I sat in that very same spot with Mose still off somewhere in the hills and me missing him and wishing I was with him and wondering why, with him so unhappy, I was feeling envious of him. I noticed that there were tears running down my face, and I was gasping for breath so that my whole body was jerking with spasms. And then I was staring at that damn door, and I felt like—and this is crazy, I know—but I felt like somehow it was all that door's fault, and, sobbing out loud by that time, I jumped up and ran over to it and picked it up. I carried it outside and heaved it just as hard as I could, screaming as I threw it. The door hung up for a second in some low-hanging branches, and as I turned and started walking toward Mose's house, I heard it fall to the ground behind me. I made it through the woods to the other cabin just on instinct, I guess, because I was crying so hard that I couldn't see, and once or twice I even walked into a tree. When I got there I stopped in front of the cabin for a short while, then I wiped my eyes so I could see better and walked around back. As soon as I rounded the back corner of the house, I saw the two little grave houses up on the hillside, and I walked straight up to them and sat down in front of them in the dirt. I guess that I didn't have any tears left by then. I just felt all empty inside, sort of like I had felt right after Jerry Smith had hit me in the stomach and I couldn't catch my breath. I sat there for a long time trying to believe that Annie was really down under there and trying to picture the little baby. I wondered if it had been a boy or a girl, and I wondered what was wrong with the world that things like this had to happen.

Then I got up and found myself walking over to the other place, where Mose used to live and where old Malachi and Henry still did. By the time I got there, I'd gotten ahold of myself fairly well again. Malachi and Henry were out in front of the cabin with a bucketful of potatoes that they had just dug up from their garden, and they were busy knocking the dirt loose from them.

" 'Siyo," I said.

Old Malachi just kind of grunted, but Henry looked up at me.

"Hi, Charlie," he said.

I felt stupid for having greeted them in Cherokee when they both knew that I couldn't really speak it but had just picked up a word here and there. I stood there in front of them awkwardly for a little while, digging the toe of my shoe into the dirt, and then I squatted down on my haunches.

"I came by because I felt like there was something I had to say to you," I said. "I mean, I ain't seen you two for a while. Not since before Mose lost his wife and the kid. And I just want to say how sorry I am. I want you to know I feel awful about it. Not as much as you, I guess, and not nearly as much as Mose, but I feel it. You know, Mose is my best friend, and he's been helping me put up my cabin so that when I get married, me and him could be neighbors. I thought that after me and Velma got married up, and, you know, had some kids of our own, that our kids would kind of grow up together, sort of the way me and Mose did, only better, because we'd all live out here in the woods close together and all that."

Old Malachi stood up with a potato in his hand. It was an ugly potato, because it had this horrible gash across its middle where the potato fork had sliced into it on its way into the ground. And he kind of grunted and pitched the thing into the bucket and turned and went into the house.

"Don't mind the old man, Charlie," said Henry. "Hell, he don't even talk much to me anymore."

"Oh, that's okay. I understand," I said, but I thought that probably old Malachi just didn't like me very much because I was too much *yoneg*.

Henry reached into the bucket and picked up that same ugly potato that Malachi had just tossed down. He pitched it up into the air and caught it again, looked at it for a couple of seconds and then looked up at me.

"What's happened to you, anyhow?" he said. "Your face is about as messed up as this here tater."

I told him the whole story, not like I had told it to Mama and Daddy and the Hotchkisses, but the whole real story about me and Velma and the graveyard, and about Jerry and Eddie, and I didn't even leave out the parts about what a lousy lover I had been, or Grandma Hotchkiss, or how much I had puked.

"We ain't going to let them get away with that shit, Charlie," Henry said.

"Wait a minute, Henry," I said. "I can't have any of this get out. I ain't told nobody the truth about last night except only you. You and me and Velma, we're the only people in the whole world who know what really happened out there."

"Me and you and Velma and them two bastard *yonegs*," he said.

"Yeah, well, anyhow, if we was to go after them to get even for what they done, then folks would find out what they done and how it all come about, don't you see?"

"Take it easy, Charlie. I understand your problem. Ain't nobody going to find out nothing about your diddling on old Granny Hotchkiss. But like I said, we ain't going to let them get away with it."

I couldn't think of any way to answer him, so I just sat there dumb while he picked up another tater and began knocking the chunks of dirt off it. Then he looked up at me, and I guess that he could see that I wasn't quite satisfied with his remarks, and he kind of grinned.

"Charlie," he said, "there's all kinds of ways of getting into a fight."

CHAPTER SIX

Monday morning Daddy and I got out of the house at the same time, which happened occasionally, and we walked on down to the store together. I was still some sore from Saturday night, but all in all, I really felt one hell of a lot better than I had the morning before. When we got to the store, I already had my keys out of my pocket and was just about ready to go up to the door first and open it for Daddy, when I happened to look up and across the street. Old Man Lawson's shop was just across from our store and down two doors, and he opened up at seven every morning just as we did. That was another thing that had been in my head all along about my cabin out in the woods. Me and Mose would not only live right there close to each other, but we would both be going in to work to practically the same place at the same time every morning. Every morning except Sunday, and if I was married and the head of my own house, then I could take my wife to church wherever the hell I felt like it, I supposed. The folks wouldn't like it much, but it didn't seem that there'd be too awful much they'd be able to do about it.

Anyway, just as I was about to go open the door, like I said, I glanced over there toward old man Lawson's shop, and there was Mose. He was standing there in the big open doorway of the blacksmith's shop in his working clothes and talking to Mr. Lawson.

"Daddy," I said, "would you go ahead and open the place up? I want to run over there a minute and see Mose."

"It's time to go to work, son. I don't want you running off somewhere with that—"

I didn't want to hear what he was going to call Mose, so I interrupted him as quickly as I could.

"I'll just be a minute," I said. "He's going to work too."

I hurried off the sidewalk and ran across the street. As I walked up behind where Mose and Lawson were standing, I could see that they were busy talking, so I didn't yell out or anything because I didn't want to interrupt them. Mose had his back to the street and to me, so he didn't see me coming up. Old Lawson did, and as I got close enough to hear what was going on, he was the one talking.

"I talked to a boy on Wednesday who told me he'd be here to go to work tomorrow. I'm sorry, Mose, but I'm running a business. I guess it ain't your fault, but that don't make things any easier on me when I don't know what's going on. I had a busy week last week, and when you didn't show up and didn't even send me no word to let me know what was wrong with you, well, I just didn't have no choice. I got me a boy coming in tomorrow morning.

"Hello, there, Charlie. How's your daddy doing?

"Mose, you just wait here a minute, and I'll bring you out the money I owe you. I don't want you to think that I'd cheat you out of what you got coming."

Old Lawson turned abruptly and walked inside the shop. I stood beside Mose feeling a little awkward and a little guilty. It occurred to me that I could have told Lawson why Mose didn't show up for work. I didn't know why I hadn't.

"Mose," I said, "I'm awful sorry about that. That old bastard ain't got a human feeling in his head. He's got no right to do that to you, not right after, well, he just ain't got the right."

"Forget it, Charlie," said Mose. "I guess he's got the right okay. It's his shop, ain't it?"

"Yeah, but Mose, hey, listen. Maybe I can talk to him."

Mose was just looking down at the street.

"No, don't do that," he said. "Just forget it. I guess I don't need a job no more anyways, do I?"

Just then Old Lawson came back out, and he handed Mose a few bills and some change. Mose took it and started to stuff it into his pocket.

"You'd better count that money, Mose," said Lawson. "Don't never let no money go in or out of your pocket without you count it."

"Aw, I trust you, Mr. Lawson."

Mose turned to leave.

"Come around when you can, Charlie," he said, "okay?"

"I'm sorry about the missus, Mose," said Lawson, turning to go back into the shop.

"Yeah, Mose, I will," I said, and I quickly turned to stop Old Lawson by grabbing him by his arm. Mose kept going.

"Hey, look, Mr. Lawson," I said, "can't you reconsider this thing? I mean, didn't Mose tell you why it was that he didn't come in last week? He was awful torn up about Annie and that kid. You can understand that, can't you?"

"Charlie, I told him I was sorry for his missus, but he didn't send me no word. These Indians don't seem to have no concept of time or no business sense. I got me a white boy coming in here tomorrow to go to work. Now, you can run on back across the street and leave me alone. Do I try to tell your daddy how to run his store?"

He went on in, and I just stood there for a minute wondering how come some folks just don't seem to have any feelings. I wondered, too, if there wasn't some way I could hurt the old son of a bitch, and then I thought about his bill at the store and how it was generally overdue. I thought that I could tell him that I was going to stop carrying him on the books, because I was learning how to be a good white businessman, and carrying him anymore on the books just didn't make good business sense. I knew, though, that I'd never get away with anything like that, because he got along real well with Daddy, and the store was all Daddy's. I just worked there, so to speak, even if Daddy always was talking about how it would all be mine one of these days, and how I had to learn to handle everything about it and to make decisions. Besides, Lawson paid his bill pretty regular, anyway, even if it was always a little late. So I just walked on back over to the store, thinking up names all the way across the street to call Old Lawson.

When I walked in the door, I hadn't even gotten it shut, when I heard Daddy real loud and kind of triumphant.

"So he was going to work too, was he?"

"He was, yeah."

"Did he really expect his job to be just sitting there waiting for him to come back to it when he felt the urge? Just what did he expect of poor Lawson, anyway?"

I clinched my teeth for an instant.

"Let's just drop the whole thing," I said.

Well, he did, but for the rest of the morning he had a very pleased look on his face no matter what it was he was doing. And to make things even worse, we had a very good day, business-wise, all day long, and he just kept getting more and more pleased until I didn't think that I could stand much more of it. I was never so glad for five o'clock to roll around as I was that evening. The two of us left the store together. I locked the door. When I turned around to join Daddy on our walk home, there was Henry just sitting on the edge of the sidewalk with his feet in the street, looking up at me and grinning.

" 'Siyo, chooj," he said, and out of the corner of my eye I saw Daddy wince. I returned his greeting, feeling real proud, but somehow, because of Daddy standing, I guess, just a little ashamed, too. Then I just stood there. I could see Daddy getting impatient with me.

"Charlie," he said, "you coming home for supper?"

What he really meant was that I had better, by God, come straight on home with him and not go out wasting time with no Indian, but I was just a little too old for him to go on saying things like that to me right out in public, and we both knew it, so for once I decided that I would take advantage of that fact.

"No," I said, feeling real bold, "I won't be home for supper. Would you mind telling Mama for me?"

Of course he would mind, but he didn't say anything more. He just turned away and started to go on home. Then I was the one feeling triumphant.

"Let's go, Henry," I said.

"Uh, inena," said Henry.

We headed down the street toward Sam Billings' place. Liquor was illegal in Indian Territory, but everyone knew where to get it, and the laws didn't bother old Sam. I guess maybe he paid them off or something. Anyhow, he had the front room of his own house fixed up kind of like a bar, and that's where we headed. Walking along, I felt pretty good for the first time in a while, and I started to tease Henry.

"You was right on the dot at five o'clock. Closing time," I said. "You sure seem to have a pretty good concept of time for an Indian."

"Hell," he said, "I been sitting on the sidewalk for more than a hour, Charlie."

We were laughing as we went into Sam Billings' place, and I paid for a bottle of whiskey. Henry took the bottle over to a table and sat down. I brought two glasses. Henry poured us each a glassful and took a long drink from his. I picked mine up and took a pretty big swallow, and it burned the hell out of my insides and made my eyes water. Henry laughed at me and took another long pull on his glass, which emptied it, and then he poured himself another one. I decided that I would take mine kind of slow after that.

"Henry," I said, "you seen Mose today?"

"Yeah."

"He tell you about that old man Lawson and his job? I mean, about him getting fired from it today?"

"Yeah."

"Well, what do you think he's going to do, Henry?"

"I guess he ain't going to go down to that damn shop at seven in the morning no more."

"But where else can he find a job?"

Henry drained his glass again, poured it full once more, then leaned back and looked at me real hard. It made me nervous, because Mose and Henry—none of the full-bloods—they almost never looked anyone in the eyes the way white folks do.

"Charlie," he said, "what the hell does Mose need with a job? Mose don't need no job. I ain't got no job. Papa ain't got no job. We ain't starving. We tend our garden and we hunt. What else do we need? We don't need money to live like white men, Charlie. I like you, *chooj*, but I'm afraid you got a little too much of your old man in you."

His last remark hurt the hell out of me, but I couldn't think of any way to defend myself against what he had said. I guess that, at least from his point of view, I did sound an awful lot like my daddy. Here I was wishing that I could be more like Henry and Mose, and yet I was all upset because Mose had lost his job—a white man's job. Maybe since I knew that I could never really be like Mose, I secretly wanted him to become more like me. Maybe that would sort of justify my own kind of life to me in some small way—if Mose saw something of value in it—and maybe because of that, I really needed Mose to have that job much more than he himself needed it. But then I reminded myself of how well he had always done in school, and how hard he had worked at learning his trade, and I thought that if I was wrong, at least maybe Henry wasn't all right either. He had never been interested in school or a job at all the way Mose had been. And all that Mose had done, all those things he had accomplished on his own in spite of his family and in the white world, those things weren't just in my head, he had done them. I was awfully confused, and the whiskey beginning to go to my head was not helping matters at all. Then Henry started talking again.

"This business with Lawson," he said, "just goes to prove that I was right all along, Charlie. Mose done real good in school, then he got him a good job. He done real good in the white way. A lot of white folks don't do as good. Am I right, Charlie?"

"Yeah, Henry, you are right about that. That's why I hate to see him just lose everything that way."

"But, Charlie, don't you see? They ain't going to let Indians do good. Not Mose or no Indian. White people don't want us doing their jobs. They don't want us to prove that we're as good as they are, to louse up their image of the lazy full-blood Indian. That's why they made us leave the old home, and that's why they're trying to take the Nation away from us now. Still, yet, Mose thought he could make it. He thought if he proved to everybody that he could get to work on time and save a little money, that he'd be accepted as being just as good as a white man. I told him it ain't going to work that way. I told him all along. He just wouldn't listen to me, but I guess he knows different now."

He poured us each another glass of whiskey and took another long drink. He was drinking about two glasses to my one, and he sure wasn't feeling the effects of it the way I was.

"Henry," I said, my tongue beginning to feel thick and clumsy in my mouth, "I'm all mixed up. I mean, I just don't think I know anything anymore. I hear what you're saying, and it all seems to make sense, but then, why the hell don't I just quit my job, you know, just walk out of the store and walk out on my old man and everything and go out in the woods the way you say?"

"Charlie, you're white. Mostly. It's like I said, you've got too much of your old man in you. The only thing that's hard to figure for me is how come you get on so well with me and Mose, how come we even like each other. I don't know."

"I ain't no goddamned *yoneg*," I said, and I drained my glass, and he poured me out another, and the bottle was empty. I leaned back in my chair so I could reach my hand in my pocket, and I pulled everything out that was in there, spilling it all out on the table in front of me. I could hardly tell what I was doing, but I did manage to separate the coins from my pocket knife and keys. I shoved the coins over toward Henry and asked him if there was enough there to get us another bottle. He said there was, counted out the proper amount and went over to the bar to get it for us. I was thinking while he was up from the table what a damn fool thing I had just done, because I was already so drunk, and I hadn't had any supper. I was afraid that I would be sick before the evening was over. Henry brought the new bottle back to the table and sat down again.

"*Wado,*" I said.

"*Howa,*" said Henry.

I had one more drink, and Henry had three. I had begun seriously to worry about how much more I could put away without getting sick, so I had slowed down a little, and he was still going at the same pace. I had just put my glass down on the table and was wanting to put my head down beside it, when Henry picked up the whiskey bottle real slow and moved it toward my face. It went right up alongside my left ear and stopped at an angle so that it was pointing back behind me toward the door. Henry was looking where he had that bottle pointed, right past my head, and he was smiling and looking kind of mean.

"Now, *chooj,*" he said, "look what's coming here. You know that sense of time you was talking about earlier? The one I ain't got? Well, I just been sitting and waiting in here, too."

I looked over my shoulder to find out what the bottle was pointing at. It was moving very slowly to follow the movements of Jerry Smith and Ed Johnson as they were going from the doorway toward the bar. My head was starting to spin.

CHAPTER SEVEN

"Henry, please . . ."

"Hey, Charlie, didn't I tell you don't worry none? Nobody's going to know nothing about nothing. We just going to have ourselves a little fight, maybe."

Jerry and Eddie bought a bottle from Sam and took a table that was, from where Henry and I were sitting, just across the open space that served as a walkway from the door to the bar. The rest of the room in front of the bar on either side of this space was filled up with tables and chairs. When Henry and I had first come in, there had been only a couple of other tables occupied, way back in the corner, but now that folks'd had time to go home and have supper, a few more customers had started to come in. Henry started talking again, and it was kind of strange, because he wasn't really talking about anything. He was usually pretty quiet unless he had something to say, and now he was talking a lot about how we hadn't gone out hunting for some time and about things me and him and Mose had done years ago and people we used to know who had gone off somewhere. He was talking loud, too, and I thought that he seemed quite a bit drunker all of a sudden, but I wondered if maybe I wasn't just so drunk by then that I didn't have much judgment left. Then Henry started laughing like he had just remembered something real funny, and he leaned across the table toward me like he had something very important to say.

"Charlie, boy," he said, "do you recall that skinny tow-headed kid used to hang around with you and Mose? Had about a hundred brothers and sisters?"

I tried very hard to remember who the hell he was talking about, and only much later when I was sober did it occur to me that there probably never had been such a kid.

"You recall the way that skinny little shit could jump through his own foot?"

"Could what? What the hell . . ."

"Aw, you remember. I mean, he could jump over his own foot. That's what I mean. Well, lookie here. I'll show you."

He stood up and took hold of his left foot in his right hand, so that he was standing there in the middle of that open space on one foot, holding on to the other one out there in front of himself, with his free arm, the left one, sticking straight out to the side to help him keep his balance, and he was kind of hopping around. He looked pretty funny, and everyone in the place was watching him. Then he got a real serious look on his face, kind of squatted down just a little bit, staring at where his right arm and left leg made a sort of hoop out there in front of him, and then he jumped straight up in the air, bringing his right foot up and over the hoop, and he came down with a hellacious loud stomp, still hanging on to his left foot with his right hand, but now they were behind him right under his ass. There was a lot of laughter from all over the room, but Henry didn't seem to notice it. He was pulling on my arm, trying to get me to stand up.

"Come on, Charlie," he said, "you try it once."

"I can't do that, Henry."

"Come on. Try it. Hell, I've drank twice as much as you, and I done it, didn't I?"

He pulled me clear up out of my chair, and I nearly fell over on him.

"Goddamn it, Henry, I can't do that. Leave me alone. I'll puke."

He let me go, and I nearly fell to the floor but managed to aim myself well enough at the chair to save myself that further embarrassment.

"Look here, Charlie," said Henry, "you can do it. It's real easy. It ain't nearly as hard as it looks."

As he finished saying this, he poured himself another full glass of whiskey and then downed it all at once, as if it was part of the preparation for his stunt. Then he set himself up for it again, just the same as before. Everyone in the room got quiet. They were watching to see if he could do it again. He did. There was much laughter again and some applause, and Henry was still standing there on one foot, hopping around to keep from falling over, holding on to his foot back there under his ass. He hopped over to the table where I was sitting, never turning loose of his foot.

"Charlie," he said, "fill up my glass for me, will you?"

I did it, and he drained it, still hopping around.

"Now, you think that was hard," he said, "you watch this next one. I'm going to take and do the same damn thing—backward."

He hopped around a little getting himself set up. All eyes in the place were on him. I think that was the quietest Billings' place had ever been with that many customers in it. Then Henry jumped straight up in the air again, about as high as he could possibly go, and as his foot started to make the trip through, it seemed like it got hung up on his other foot where he was holding it. He seemed to be suspended there in midair for a few seconds, although, of course, I know it couldn't have been as long as it seemed to me, but while he was up there with his legs all tangled up, I noticed that he was directly in front of and above where Jerry Smith was sitting with his chair turned away from the table so he could watch all the fun. Well, the way Henry was trying to jump, he had thrown his weight back some, and when he came down, it was right in Jerry's lap, and with such force that the right rear leg of Jerry's chair snapped off, and Jerry and Henry went over backward. It was such a crash that I thought Jerry would have a couple of broken ribs at least, but he didn't. He was hurt a little, I guess, but mostly he was mad. He was yelling as loud as he could to Henry, who seemed to be trying very hard to untangle himself and get up from on top of Jerry.

"Get off of me, you goddamn drunk Indian," Jerry said. "Someone get this drunk son of a bitch off of me. Eddie."

Eddie was laughing so hard that it took him a while to get up and around to where he could help. He grabbed ahold of Henry by an arm and pulled to help him stand. Henry was straining real hard as he was pulling against Eddie's arm and slowly getting up, and just as he was only to about a half-standing position, with his ass right in Jerry's face, he let an awful fart. I knew that he had always been able to do that about any time he wanted to, and then I couldn't help myself anymore, and I started laughing, too. I don't think anyone noticed me, though, because the whole damn place was in an uproar. Jerry came to his feet as fast as he could as soon as Henry was out of his way. He was shaking with rage and red in the face, as he kicked the pieces of broken chair out from under his feet.

"I sure hope you ain't hurt," Henry was saying. "I'm awful sorry."

Jerry's fist shot out real fast and caught Henry alongside of the head. It was just a glancing blow, but it knocked him off balance some, and he stepped back a couple of steps, catching himself by putting his hand down on the table right next to me. The place got real quiet again.

"You dirty, stinking son of a bitch," said Jerry.

Sam Billings raised a shotgun up from behind the bar and pointed it in the general direction of where the four of us, me, Henry, Jerry and Eddie, were. It wouldn't have taken any more careful of an aim than that. A few people who thought that they might be too close to the pattern hurried out of the way, moving back into the corners of the room.

"I think that boy's looking for a fight, Sam," said Henry. "You heard me apologize to him, didn't you? Look, boy, I don't want no fight. What you have to go and hit me for?"

"I think you done that on purpose, you goat shit," said Jerry. "Nobody does that to me and gets away with it. I'm going to stomp you. . . ."

"Outside," came Sam's voice from behind the shotgun.

"Sam says, 'outside,' boy."

Henry said that last as he was lifting Jerry up off the floor by his shirtfront, and, all in one motion, he turned and ran the few steps to the door, throwing Jerry through it and out into the street. And Henry was out there right behind him. As Sam put the gun back under the bar, every man in the place was up and on the way to the door to watch the fight. Eddie, having the spot nearest the door, excluding me, was the first one out behind Henry. I thought that I would be next, but I was nearly trampled by the crowd, I was so damned wobbly on my feet, so I wound up being the last one out there. The crowd stopped outside without clearing the doorway, and I had a hell of a time getting out at all. I was trying desperately to sober up, because I figured that Henry would have both of those two on his tail and probably needed my help, but it was hopeless. When I had finally gotten myself through the crowd and out where I could see, Henry had already laid out Eddie Johnson, who was down in the dirt holding his guts and gasping for breath.

"Go get Foster," I heard someone say, and then I heard someone running down the sidewalk on the other side of the mob from where I was, going in the direction of the deputy marshal's office. I thought that I'd better try to stop Henry before Deputy Foster got there, and I stepped off the sidewalk and down into the street, but my head started to spin like it was going to spin right off. To keep from falling over on my face, I relaxed my legs and just sat straight down. I didn't really sit, I fell—but I did it in a sitting position. I heard a loud crack or two when someone was getting hit hard, but I couldn't seem to hold my head up, and the crowd was so damned loud. Then the noise stopped, not all at once, but it got much quieter.

"By God," someone said, "he whupped them both."

I raised my head up to see, and Eddie was still where he had been the first time I looked, but now Jerry was lying flat on his back right out in the middle of the street—out cold. Henry was standing there beside him with his back to me and the rest of the crowd, and he had his head down and his hands were in front of him. My head was fuzzy, but I remember thinking that it was strange that he would be praying at a time like that, and for those two especially.

"What the hell's he doing?" somebody said.

Then the stream shot out and we all knew. A man standing behind me let out a loud guffaw.

"Goddamn," he said. "He's pissing on that old boy."

And it was just at that time that Deputy Foster walked up behind Henry with a long-barreled pistol and laid it across the top of Henry's head. Henry crumpled up right beside Jerry and just kept peeing—all over himself. Everyone started laughing again, and most of them went back inside Sam's place. Foster yelled at someone from the sidewalk to come over and help him. He watched Henry until he was satisfied that it would be safe and dry to do anything with him, and then the two men grabbed hold of Henry's arms and started dragging him down the street toward the jail. The newly appointed helper jerked his head back toward the other two near-lifeless shapes in the street.

"What about them two, Deputy?" he said.

"They ain't hurt bad, are they?"

"Naw, I don't think so."

"Then someone throw some water in their face and send them on home," said Foster.

That last had been said loud and was in the nature of a general order, and somebody who hadn't yet gone back inside carried it out. I wasn't paying attention anymore, though. The fight was over, Henry was on his way to jail, and I didn't give a goddamn for those two. I was just wishing real hard that I could be home in bed so I could try to sleep off that drunk. But even though it was well after dark, it was still too early for my folks to be in bed. I couldn't very well go staggering into the house in front of them like the very devil, drunk and stinking, and there was no way I would be able to get into bed without them seeing me. I couldn't just keep on sitting there on the main street of town like an ordinary drunk, though. I had to do something. I thought about going out to see Mose and telling him all about what had happened and staying out there until it was late enough for me to go home. The only problem with that idea was that in the shape I was in, I wasn't sure that I would ever even make it all the way out to his place. Then I thought about Velma.

"Good old Velma," I said out loud, but to no one but myself. "She is good for something else after all."

I pulled myself up from the sidewalk and stood there for a few seconds to get myself used to the change in altitude, and then I started to walk, very slowly, toward Velma's house. I had to stop twice before I got there and just lean on the nearest wall and let my head spin a bit, but I did get to her house without passing out or even having to stop and puke, and I was thankful for even that small blessing. I walked up to the front of the yard, and then I stopped and wondered why in God's name I had gone there. I couldn't any more go in there like I was than I could go in my own house. If anything, it would be even dumber. I couldn't even go up and knock on the door and ask Velma to come outside with me, because one of her folks might answer, and they'd be sure to notice the reek. I decided just to sit down under an old tree out there on the edge of their yard in the dark and watch the house, and maybe old Velma would come out in the yard for some reason, and then I could get her attention without her folks' ever seeing me. There were just all kinds of reasons a girl might want to go outside on a night like that one, I thought, and the more I thought about it, the more certain I was that it would happen like that. It kind of made sense that two people who are in love would sometimes get their thoughts all tangled together, maybe even without knowing it. And if I was out there really wanting to see her, maybe somehow she would know about it, or maybe she wouldn't exactly know about it, but something inside her would make her go out in the yard. And there I would be, and then she would know what it had been that made her do it.

I sat there under that tree thinking about all that, the whole time just on the verge of falling asleep—or passing out, I'm not sure which —and about midnight I got up and walked home.

CHAPTER EIGHT

Needless to say, Tuesday morning in the store was a very uncomfortable one for me. I had a terrible hangover and had to do my best to conceal it from Daddy, which only served to make it worse, and on top of that, I was constantly worrying about Henry. As was bound to happen, a customer came into the store about midmorning—it was George Sweet, the photographer, a friend of Daddy's—and told Daddy the whole story about the big fight he had seen at Sam Billings' place last night. My heart was pounding so hard that I was afraid they would hear it and ask me what was wrong, but luck was with me. After all, I hadn't been involved in the fight, not in any way that anyone could see. Henry had kept his word about that. Of course, Daddy knew that I had been with Henry, and then loudmouth Sweet turned to me once in the middle of his story.

"You were there, Charlie," he said. "You saw how Henry Pathkiller took on both of those boys out in the street."

And I just nodded, trying to avoid Daddy's glance. Finally Sweet left.

"Well, Charlie," said Daddy.

"Yes?"

"I knew you shouldn't have gone out with him, and if you'd just be honest with me, and with yourself, I'm sure that you'd admit the same thing. I think you knew better."

"Yeah. Well, you're probably right."

"I want you to know, when George began telling me about that fight last night, and when I heard him say 'Henry Pathkiller,' I was worried half sick."

"Aw, Daddy . . ."

Here he reached out and put his hand on my shoulder, and I felt real uncomfortable. I wished that he would move his hand. In fact, I wished that he wasn't even there, or that I was somewhere else. I felt just a little guilty about the way that I was feeling too, because, after all, he is my daddy.

"I just can't tell you," he said, "how relieved I was when he had finished the whole thing and I was sure that you hadn't been involved. For that part, I'm grateful, and I'm proud of you, son. We won't say anything to your mama about this affair."

"No," I said, but I was wondering if I would ever be able to be proud of myself again for anything. If only he had known just how involved I really was, how the whole thing had happened because of me, and how I hadn't been able to help Henry any. The door opened to stop the conversation, and I was damned glad of it. I looked up to see who it was coming in and saw that it was Velma.

"Well, good morning, Velma," said Daddy. "What can we do for you this morning?"

"Good morning, Mr. Black. Hi, Charlie. I've got this list of things, Mr. Black, to pick up for Mama, but I'm afraid that I couldn't possibly get all that stuff all the way back home by myself. I don't know what in the world Mama must have been thinking about, sending me after all that."

She handed him the list.

"Well," he said, "let's see what we need here."

"I don't suppose you could spare little old Charlie here for just long enough to help me carry all that heavy stuff home, Mr. Black."

"Oh, I reckon that I might be able to hold down the fort by myself long enough to let him do that, Velma."

I started helping him to fill the order she had brought in.

"I'll be happy to carry this stuff home for you," I said.

"I understand there was just an awful fight in town last night."

"That's right," said Daddy.

"Henry Pathkiller was fighting Jerry Smith and Eddie Johnson both at the same time?"

"Yup. That's what I heard."

"They say that Henry Pathkiller is down at the jailhouse right this very minute for it."

"Is that right?" said Daddy. "Well, that's the place for him. Drunk and brawling in the streets."

"I certainly do think you're right about that, Mr. Black. Why, that's an awful way for a grown man to behave. Henry must be 'most nearly thirty years old."

"Well, I'm sure he is, Velma. At least that. But, you know, these backwoods Indians just can't seem to adjust to the times. They can't hold a job, and anytime they come into town, they get to drinking and usually end up starting a fight. Maybe he'll cool off a little in jail, although I doubt it."

He had just put the last item on Velma's list into a bag, and he shoved the bag down the counter toward me.

"I'll get it all down on the bill, Charlie," he said. "You go on ahead."

I didn't miss the smug look he gave me, and I figured I knew what it meant, but I just picked up the bag, and Velma and I left the store. I was glad that she had come by, but it wasn't so much that I wanted to see her. It was more that she gave me an excuse to get out of there, but once we were outside, she started jabbering at me.

"Charlie," she said, "did you have anything to do with Henry Pathkiller beating up those two last night?"

Damn, I thought, Daddy in the store and Velma out. I can't get away from it anywhere.

"No," I said. "I was there, and I saw it, but no. What would I have to do with it, anyhow?"

"Well, it's just such a coincidence. I thought maybe you went and told him about that night out there, and he maybe decided to help you to even or something."

"Velma, believe me, it was just a coincidence. I wouldn't tell anyone about us. You know that. I mean, it's just too personal and everything. It means too much to me. You ought to know that."

"Well, I certainly did hope so, Charlie, but it did seem kind of strange. You can't blame me for asking, now, can you?"

I could, and I did, in spite of the fact that she had figured it exactly right and I had been lying to her, but I lied once more and reassured her that the whole thing had happened almost by accident. In order to really convince her that I wasn't lying about it, I told her exactly how it had happened—that is, how it looked to anyone who didn't know what was really happening. She finally seemed to be convinced, and she even allowed herself a small titter at the thought of Henry peeing on Jerry Smith.

"Well, Charlie," she said, "I don't really care who did it, but if it's for sure not going to get us into trouble, then I'm certainly glad that somebody taught those two dreadful boys a lesson. I only hope that they don't decide to say anything about us just because they know you're a friend of his."

"Velma, we went all through this before. Remember? They can't afford to have anyone knowing about that night any more than we can. Not now any more than before."

"Oh, I'm sure you're right, Charlie. I just worry too much, I guess."

"I am right about this, Velma," I said. "I really don't blame you for worrying about it some, though. It would be a pretty awful thing for you if word did get out. But look, once we get married, it won't be anybody's business what we do. Or what we've done, for that matter. And you won't have to worry about it anymore."

"Charlie," she said, "I can hardly wait. Why do we have to wait any longer? Let's go ahead and get married right away, Charlie."

I realized too late that I'd gotten myself in trouble. I didn't really want that subject brought up.

"I've got to finish that cabin," I said, "so we'll have a place to live, and I need to save up a little more money. I want to feel like I can take real good care of you before I ask you to be my wife."

"Oh, I know that, Charlie, but can't you hurry it up a little? You know, I just don't think I'll ever be able to go out to that old graveyard again after what happened out there, and if we don't have anyplace to go, well, I just don't know how long I'll be able to stand it, Charlie."

She said the one thing that I could agree with. She sure did know my weakness. I've got to give her that.

"I know, Velma," I said. "I feel the same way."

And for once, I wasn't lying to her.

When I left Velma at her house, I hurried as fast as I could, because I had decided that I would stop by the jail and see if Henry was all right or if he was in any kind of real trouble. I didn't want Daddy to know about it, so I had to get back to the store as quickly as possible. I stopped outside the door to the deputy marshal's office just long enough to catch my breath, and then I went inside.

"Hello, Charlie. What can I do for you?"

"Hello, Mr. Foster. I just stopped by to ask about Henry Pathkiller."

"Well, he's in there, all right," said Foster, nodding his head over his shoulder toward the back where the cells were.

"What's he charged with, Mr. Foster?"

"Oh hell, I guess he ain't really charged with anything, Charlie. He was just drunker than hell last night, and he beat up two white boys. There don't seem to be no clear idea how the fight got started, and I guess they was drunk, too. Anyhow, they ain't offered to come in here and make no formal complaint against old Henry, so I just sort of got him in here to let him sober up. Maybe teach him a little lesson. Maybe next time he wants to fight with a white man, maybe he'll think about it first. He could get himself in a lot of trouble that way, you know. Even when the Cherokees had their own courts back a few years ago, even then, Indian offenses against a white man went to federal court."

"Yeah, I know," I said.

"I could charge him with liquor violation, but then, there was a bunch of them drunk last night."

He gave me a knowing look, as if to say that he knew that I was one of them. I was thinking that Sam Billings probably paid Foster to leave him alone with his illegal saloon, and Foster didn't want to get anything stirred up that would naturally lead to Billings.

"Has he been in long enough, you think?" I asked.

"You asking me to let him out, Charlie?"

"Well, yeah. I guess. If you can."

"I suppose he's been in there about long enough. Here."

With his last word, he tossed me a big key ring.

"Thanks, Mr. Foster," I said, and I hurried through the back door to the cells. Henry was in the very first cell. Weeknights were usually pretty quiet. I put the key in the lock and turned it. Henry heard the noise of the lock being turned and looked up from the cot he was on.

"Charlie," he said. "You finally wake up, did you?"

"You smell like one stinking Indian," I said as I opened the door.

"You breaking me out of jail, or Foster give you those keys?"

"It's okay. Foster give me the keys."

"Shit," said Henry. "I was kind of hoping you was breaking me out."

As we walked through the door into the outer office, I gave Foster back the keys and thanked him again.

"Thanks for the night's lodging, innkeeper," said Henry.

"Henry," said Foster, his voice tired, "learn to watch yourself around town, you hear? Next time, you might not be so lucky as you was last night. You might find yourself in big trouble one of these days you keep that stuff up. You might go too far, or there might be a deputy here who's not as easygoing as me."

"I understand you, Mr. Marshal, sir. I understand. Don't worry none about old Henry. He just appreciates the decent way you treated him and the use of the fine facilities. Thank you, sir."

"Get out of here," said Foster.

We got out, and it was none too soon for me.

"Henry, you damn fool," I said.

"We sure got them last night, didn't we, Charlie, boy?"

"Yeah," I said. "We sure as hell did."

Out in the open air, Henry's stink was even more noticeable than it had been in the jail cell where it had at least been mixed with the stink of a hundred other drunks from a hundred other nights and had become a permanent part of the walls and the floor of the building. But once we got outside, he even began to smell himself.

"You know, Charlie," he said, "I think I better get out of this town and back out to my house so I can clean up and change my clothes. I smell bad. You want to come along out to the house with me, Charlie?"

I told him that I had to get back to work, and we parted company. I was real relieved to find out that it was so easy to get him out of jail, and I was glad to know that he was leaving town, too. I went back to the store, and nothing unusual at all came up the rest of the day. Even my headache had finally gone away, and it looked like the whole mess was over and done.

CHAPTER NINE

The rest of that week passed without much of any significance occurring. I had no problems with Velma other than the fact that she was getting much more anxious for us to set a date for the wedding. She was scared to go back to the graveyard too, and under any other circumstances, that would have been a big problem for me too. I had too many other problems on my mind that particular week, though, for that to have bothered me too much. I had supper with the Hotchkisses one night that week—I think it was on Thursday. I'm not really sure. Daddy was even careful not to mention either Mose or Henry by name, although it would have been asking way too much of him to think that he might go for a period of time that long without carrying on some about lazy full-bloods. I'd gotten so used to that, however, that I hardly even heard what he was saying anymore. I didn't see either Mose or Henry all the rest of that week, and I didn't see Jerry or Eddie around anywhere either.

Friday I went calling on Velma after supper time. She got off on the same old topic. When would we set a date? Why wasn't I hurrying things up any?

"Charlie," she said, "I've agreed to go live with you out in that silly old cabin. That's what you wanted, isn't it? Well, I told you that we could go out there to live. I said that, didn't I? It's what you wanted. Can't you hurry up and get it ready for us?"

What she had actually told me earlier, just for the record, was that she'd give it a try for a while, but it was obvious right from the beginning that she wasn't going to give any consideration to actually thinking about making a home out there. But I figured two can play at that game. Once we got out there in the cabin, I figured, why, there's just no telling how long it might take me to save up enough to get a place in town. Oh, I knew that she would win eventually, but I thought that I would be able to keep us out there quite a bit longer than she expected. I didn't want to bring any of this up, though, because I just wasn't in any mood for arguments and such. So to quiet Velma down, I told her that I would go out to the cabin first thing in the morning. I was sure that Daddy'd let me have the morning off, if he knew the reason, and I'd hang up that old door, and I'd start to put some furniture in the place. I'd work on it the whole weekend, and then Sunday evening or Monday we could go out and take a look at it and see if we both thought that it was in shape for us to move in. I didn't want to say anything definite about dates yet, so I made it sound like we really needed that work done over the weekend before we could decide what the date would be. I figured it at least partly right, because she got just about as excited as if we had set the date and made all the arrangements, and I felt like I had gained myself a little more time of relaxation before I really had to start thinking about it again.

I explained everything to Daddy when I got home that night, and he agreed, and Mama got all excited. Then both of them started thinking about what I could have from the house and from the store to help outfit the cabin. There were a couple of old chairs in the house that Mama had been wanting to get rid of anyway, and this was a good opportunity. I would have to do a little work on them to make them look nice again, but other than that, they were as good as ever. There was a table down at the store, sitting way back at the back, which Daddy said I could take because we never really used it for anything, he said. We did use it, but I didn't argue with him. I decided that the bed would have to be the last thing to be moved in. We were going to take Velma's bed out of her room at her folks' house. They had bought her a nice big one a while back and told her that when she got married, she could take it with her, so it couldn't very well be moved out to the cabin until she was.

I got up Saturday morning as usual and had breakfast with the folks. Then, when Daddy went to open up the store, I went down to the livery stable and rented me a wagon and a couple of horses. I loaded those old chairs and that table and a few other odds and ends into the wagon, and, though I'm not sure why I did it, I put my hunting rifle under the seat, along with a brand-new box of shells that I had picked up while I was in the store to get the table. Then I drove out to the cabin.

I never had been one to do much hard work by myself, and what I did that morning was I just kind of fooled around, messing with one thing for a while and then with another. But I did get the wagon unloaded, and I actually got that goddamned door hung up on hinges, after I went out and picked it up from where it had lain ever since I had thrown it out there. I drove the wagon back into town around noon and turned it in and paid for it. Then, after I'd had some lunch at home, I started to walk back out to the cabin. The only thing was, when I got out that direction a ways, I found myself walking, not on over to my place, but straight to Mose's. It was damn near a week since I'd promised him that I'd come around, and I felt a little guilty about not having kept my promise earlier. Besides that, I just wanted to see him.

When I got there, Mose was nowhere to be seen, and the place looked like it hadn't been used for a while. I thought about it, and it made sense to me that he wouldn't want to be around the old place with Annie up there on the hill instead of down in the cabin. Then I walked on over to old Malachi's cabin, and sure enough, there they were, all three. Old Malachi just kind of grunted at me, like he always did, but Mose and Henry both seemed real glad to see me. We walked out in the woods just a little ways and sat down to talk. I found out that Henry had filled Mose in on all that had happened leading up to his night in jail, and then the two of us, me and Henry, rehashed some of the events, and all of us had some good laughs over it. Mose laughed about as much as me or Henry, but somehow, and I really can't say what it was, but somehow I got the feeling that inside, Mose was taking the whole thing much more seriously than either of us were.

After we had spent some time like that, I told them about my latest episode with Velma, and how I was really supposed to be over there at my cabin right that very minute, working away to bring the big day just that much closer.

"Why didn't you say that before?" said Mose. "Me and Henry can go on down there and help you get the job done."

"How you like the way he volunteers me so fast for work?" said Henry.

"Aw," I said, "you don't neither one of you have to do that. I didn't come up here to try to get myself some workers. I just come up here to talk some."

"I know we don't need to do that, Charlie," said Mose, "but we can. Let's go."

"You ain't going to try to stop us, are you?" said Henry.

"Okay," I said. "On one condition. I bet you that the three of us together get more work done by tonight than I'd do by myself the whole damn weekend. Right?"

"Maybe so," said Mose.

"Well, it just happens that I got a whole brand-new box of .30-.30 shells down there in my cabin, and if we work, the three of us, the rest of today, why, hell, we can just take off bright and early in the morning and go hunt all day."

"Charlie, you just made a deal," said Henry.

As it turned out, I was right. The three of us working the rest of that Saturday got much more done than I would have in two full days working alone. We bedded down on the floor of my cabin for the night, and we got up with the dawn, taking our rifles and my box of shells. We kept going all day and ate parched corn to keep ourselves moving. At the end of the day, we had a mess of squirrels, a few quails, and a rabbit, and we had us a regular feast. It was about the best day that I'd had in a long, long time. I wished that it would never end, but of course it did, and that a hell of a lot sooner than I felt like it should. Then I started home, thinking about how I had a whole week to look forward to with nothing but parents, mine and Velma's, the store and customers, and nothing for relief but Velma and her constant talking. I thought that I'd have to find some kind of substitute for the graveyard or I wouldn't be able to stand the damn town much longer. I mean, what else was there to do down there?

I went on home and found Mama and Daddy both still up, and I told them what all I'd accomplished in my two days out at the cabin, meaning what all Mose and Henry and me had done in half a day, and they were very impressed and told me how proud they were of me. Then they started talking about Velma and her family, and how they were both so pleased with the plans for the wedding, and how sure they both were that I was doing the right thing.

CHAPTER TEN

Monday after work I walked over to Velma's house and picked her up. She had prepared a basket of food for us, like for a picnic. Her parents told us not to be gone too long, and we left for the cabin. While I had been working during the day, I had come up with this really great idea. I thought that I would take off for a few minutes from the store, just long enough to run over and talk to Velma. I would tell her that I had gotten a lot done on the cabin over the weekend and ask her if she didn't want to walk out and take a look at it when I got off work. She could tell me anything that maybe I had overlooked that a woman who's thinking about setting up housekeeping in a place would notice right away, and between the two of us we could figure out just what all still needed doing. With the wedding getting to be more and more a reality to everybody, and with all of them besides me getting very anxious for a definite date, it wasn't very difficult to arrange. Daddy was happy to give me the few minutes off, and Velma's Mama went for the idea right away. Needless to say, so did Velma, and she came up with the idea of the picnic basket, so we wouldn't have to waste any daylight staying in town long enough to have supper. The only problem connected with the whole plan came up when Mrs. Hotchkiss expressed a desire to go along and see the place for herself, so that she could offer us the benefit of her hundred or so years of housekeeping experience. I was certainly thankful when Velma took care of that for us by telling her old lady that she wanted to see the place first just with me, so that we would be able to put everything together by ourselves and then show off what we had done. She said at least we would be able to tell them exactly what we had planned, even if it wasn't all finished when they went out to see it a little later on. That apparently made good enough sense, so that Mrs. Hotchkiss not only agreed to wait a bit but made a little apology for even having suggested such a thing.

When we got out to the cabin, I could see it in her face right away that she really didn't like it one goddamn bit, but I knew also that she was pretty concerned with getting me to make that final commitment, so she had to tread a fine line. We went inside, and I guess the place did look a real mess, but, after all, we were still working on it.

"Well, Charlie," she said, "it does need a good cleaning up, and it needs some curtains. But I guess we could make a home out of this—for a while, I mean."

Her attitude would have upset me quite a bit if not for the fact that I had known all along exactly what her reaction to the cabin would be. I was pretty proud of that cabin, but I knew what kind of life Velma was used to, and I knew what her likes and dislikes were. I couldn't help but give her a little credit, though, for trying so hard not to show what she really felt about the place.

"Anyway, Charlie, it will be ours. There won't be anybody to bother us out here, and we'll be able to do whatever we want just anytime we feel like it. It'll be a nice-enough place for us—until we can get something better in town."

She knew what she was saying, and she knew how I felt about it. As soon as she got those last words out of her mouth, she had turned and put her arms around me and pulled me real close to her, pressing our bodies hard together. Besides the fact that I just didn't want any arguments about anything—well, that just didn't seem like the time to start one. I was thinking how nice she felt all over, and how alone we were, and how much time we had, and was just about to make some kind of suggestion based on those observations, when she pulled away from me and ran over to where I had put the picnic basket down on the old table I had hauled out from the store.

"Are you hungry, Charlie?" she said. "I'm just starved."

"I'm not really starving, but I guess I could eat something."

"Well, here. Help me spread this cloth out on the table."

"Why don't we go outside and have a real picnic?"

"Oh, Charlie. I want to sit here at our table."

I said okay and helped her spread out the damn cloth. We ate. Then we fooled around for a little, talking about what I needed to do with the cabin before we could move in. She probably would have made many more suggestions than she did, except that she was in a hurry for me to get the job done. I think that she knew the state of the cabin was my single biggest excuse for putting off the wedding.

"You remember," I said, "what you said while ago about this place?"

"What?"

"That if nothing else, that at least there won't be anybody out here to bother us?"

"Oh, yeah. Well?"

"Well, there's nobody to bother us right now," I said.

I started to pull her down to the floor. It was just a dirt floor, and she started to protest right away, but just as I was about to become very angry with her, I saw that she was taking the cloth off of the table and spreading it out on the floor. I sat down on the cloth, looking up at her and waiting for her to sit down beside me. Instead, she strolled over to the door and dropped the wooden latch down into place and walked back over to where I was sitting. Then she really surprised me. Instead of sitting on down beside me, she stood there in front of me, smiling her wicked smile down at me, and started to take off her clothes—all of them. Always before, we'd been in the graveyard, not feeling too secure, and we'd just pulled up her dress and down my breeches. I'd never seen Velma like that before, and it got me so excited that I was afraid I was going to slobber all over myself. In fact, I'd never seen any girl like that before, except once me and Mose had slipped up on Henry and Sarah out in the woods when we were just kids. But that wasn't the same as this. Sarah had been mostly covered up by Henry at the time, and we hadn't been very close to them, and I was really too young at the time, anyway. But Velma was just standing there right in front of my face completely naked, and we were all alone. When I was finally able to take my eyes off her long enough to move, I got up and undressed too, and then we both lay down on the cloth together. It was so different. It was almost like we were doing it for the first time, and I forgot all about all those reasons I'd had earlier for being mad at her.

It was just about sundown when Velma and I were walking down the main street of town headed toward her house. Before we got to the corner where we would have turned off, we noticed a fairly large crowd gathering on the sidewalk just in front of Foster's office. There was a wagon out in the street. The people in the crowd were bumping and pushing against each other, trying to get better positions for something or other, and it sounded, from where we were, like everybody was talking at the same time.

"What do you suppose that's all about, Charlie?" Velma said.

"I don't know. You want to go take a look?"

We hurried on down to where they were, so we wouldn't miss out on any more of whatever was happening than we had to, and just as we got there, Foster was yelling at the crowd to quiet down and spread out some. I could see that the wagon belonged to that Mr. Motl, who had moved out here a few months back with his family. They were immigrants from someplace in Europe, but I was never quite sure just where, and he was trying to farm a little piece of land just east of town. There wasn't much to farm yet, because he was still busy clearing the rocks away and probably would be for some time to come. He only came into town once every month, and he always came in his wagon and brought his wife and three kids. He always came early in the morning and was gone again by noon. I didn't see any sign of the rest of his family, and I remembered having seen him just about a week earlier, when he had come into the store for some supplies. Everyone in town thought that he was funny, mainly because of the way he talked, but they all pretty much agreed that he was a very fine and upstanding man and a very hard worker.

"All right now," Foster was saying, "everyone just quiet down so we can find out something here. All right, now. Shut up."

Just at that time, Velma and I managed to poke ourselves in between some of the people in the crowd so we could get a look up on the sidewalk, and there was Jerry Smith and Eddie Johnson all laid out on the sidewalk just as nice as you please, right side by side. They looked kind of stiff, and their clothes were all dirty. Someone had folded their arms up on their chests, and their heads were propped up just a little against the wall of Foster's office. Their mouths were opened slightly, and whoever it was that had been so careful about their arms hadn't bothered to close their eyes. There was blood all over both shirts, but a lot more on Jerry. Their boots were missing. Velma grabbed on to my arm real hard.

"Oh my God, Charlie," she said.

I thought that I should take her away from there, but we were both frozen to the spot, and we kept staring at the bodies. I was thinking how up until that very minute, I would have wished them both dead, but looking at them there, I just felt sick. Foster started to talk to Mr. Motl.

"How'd you happen to come across them, Mr. Motl?" he said.

"I vas taking rocks from off my land," said Motl. "I must take vagon and go few miles avay, up de road toovard town to trow rocks out, yah? It vas ven I pull to side of road to look ver I vill trow rocks avay. Den I see dese two. Dey vas in booshes. Chust trown down hill, I tink."

"Just throwed off the side of the road, huh? You see anything else unusual around anywhere?"

"No, I don't tink so. I only look around kvickly, dough. I tink I better get dem in here to you. Det vas right, yah?"

"Yeah, Mr. Motl," said Foster. "You done the right thing."

I turned to the man standing beside me.

"What happened to them?" I said.

"Shot in the back. Both of them."

"Mr. Motl," Foster said, "you can go on back home now, if you want. We'll take care of things from here. If I ride out to your place first thing in the morning, you reckon you can show me just where you found these boys?"

"Same place I alvays trow rocks. I can show you. I hope you find who do dese ting."

Motl turned slowly and went back to his wagon. He climbed back into the driver's seat, then he turned toward Foster.

"I vill be home in de morning until you are coming, Mr. Foster."

He flicked his reins, and the wagon started to roll on its way back out of town. Then there was a terrific powder flash, and a horse that was tied up right nearby started to whinny and stomp around, pulling on his reins. I hadn't noticed him until that happened, but George Sweet had set his camera up right at the feet of the two bodies, and that flash was him taking a picture of them from down there looking right into their faces. Somebody came up bringing Prang, the undertaker.

"What happened to them?" said Prang.

"Shot in the back," said Foster. "Leastwise, Johnson was. Looks to me like Johnson and Smith was walking along the road together, and someone come up behind them with a rifle, aiming to get them both. Shot Johnson clean through the heart from the backside. He was the lucky one. Looks like when he heard the shot, Smith started to turn around, and the next shot caught him in the shoulder. Another one caught him in the stomach. Last one probably in the neck. Anyhow, that's the way I figure it. Them's where the shots hit."

"It don't look like they was carrying no guns," someone said.

"I never knowed them to," said Foster.

"Cold-blooded murder," said Sweet.

"Who'd a-done a thing like this?"

"There ain't much telling right now."

Foster looked at Prang.

"Can you take care of them, Jud?"

"I'll handle it."

"The rest of you folks move on out of here now. Ain't nothing more to see here. Go on back where you come from."

I took Velma around her shoulders and turned her away from the sidewalk.

"Come on," I said. "Let's go."

"Well," she said in a real low voice, "we won't have to worry about anything they might say anymore."

But before I'd had time to reflect on Velma's cold-blooded comment, I heard Sam Billings' voice behind us talking to Foster.

"I don't know if I ought to bring this up or not, Deputy," he said, "but, well, you recall how Henry Pathkiller had that big fight with these boys over at my place the other night?"

I looked over my shoulder and saw Foster staring off into space like he was studying something real hard.

"Yeah, Sam," he said. "I just been thinking on that."

CHAPTER ELEVEN

"Wait up just a minute, Velma," I said, and I ran back to where Foster was standing. Sam had already turned to go back to his place, where most of the crowd had headed when Foster sent them away.

"Mr. Foster," I said, "you don't really think that Henry did this, do you?"

"Well, now, Charlie," said Foster, "I can't rightly be sure of nothing at this time, now can I?"

"I guess you can't, Mr. Foster, but, well, I know Henry almost like a brother, and I just know that he wouldn't do a thing like this."

"Charlie," said Foster, in that tired voice he used so much, "fifteen or twenty people seen Henry stomp them two boys the other night and then commence to piss on them. Some of them says Henry started the fight. Some says that Smith did. All I know is I finished it by cracking Henry on the skull and hauling his ass down to jail for the night and half the next morning. Men sometimes holds grudges, you know. There've been killings for less reason than that fight, Charlie. And he might feel like they had it coming, seeing as how he was the one had to set in the jailhouse. Especially, now, if it happened that they really was the ones started the fight."

I thought about telling Foster that Henry had started it, that I knew he had started it and how he had started it, that he had whipped them and was satisfied. But Velma was standing right over there waiting for me, and I knew that I couldn't tell the story. I wanted to tell it real bad, but I just couldn't get myself to bring it out.

"Mr. Foster," I said, "Henry just wouldn't have done it. Not like that. And besides that, why, anybody could've done it. Robbers. I remember there was a man shot over at the edge of the Creek Nation a few weeks back. Maybe the same ones did this."

"Could be, Charlie. You just relax and let me do my job, all right? I ain't about to go out and arrest a man for murder or go shooting at him without I know I got the right man. I'm just thinking that Henry had a motive, and I got to start my investigation somewhere. I'll go out and talk to Henry tomorrow. Maybe just bring him in for questioning. You understand?"

"Yeah, I guess so," I said.

I was starting to walk back to Velma when Foster shouted after me.

"If he ain't guilty," he said, "he ain't got nothing to worry about, Charlie."

I took Velma on home, and then I started right back out of town on the same trail I had just come in on, but when I got outside of town a ways, I turned and headed for old Malachi's place. I had to let Henry know what had happened. I didn't know what good it was going to do, if any, but I thought that he needed to know at least, so he wouldn't be thrown off guard by Foster showing up out there all unexpected-like. If he was surprised by Foster, he might act like he was guilty or something. And, I suppose, way back in my mind, although I wouldn't admit it to myself for anything, was the thought that maybe Henry had killed those two, and, if he had, he would need to know that the bodies had been found and that he was suspected.

I found the three Pathkillers all at home in the cabin. They were a little surprised to see me out there late on a weeknight, but I told them that I had a real special reason for being there. Then I asked Henry if Mose and old Malachi knew everything there was to know about me and him and Jerry Smith and Eddie Johnson. He said that they did. Then I told them how I had come out to my cabin with Velma, and how when we had gone back into town, there was Mr. Motl with his wagon. And I told them what Mr. Motl had hauled into town. I was a little disappointed at their reaction, or rather, lack of one, to my story. I thought it was pretty exciting news, and they just sat there. Henry didn't seem at all surprised, and I wondered if maybe he had done it. But then, Mose and Malachi were just sitting there, too. I thought that maybe Henry had done it and had told them about it, but I shook that thought out of my head. I didn't want to believe it, and I felt bad for even thinking it. I guess that my mind was just so bothered by everything that was going on around me that I was reading a lot into everything I saw. Finally Henry spoke up.

"Well, Charlie," he said, "I can't think of two nicer white men for such a thing to happen to."

"Henry," I said, "you don't understand. I didn't come all the way back out here just to carry news. That could have waited. I come out here because Foster thinks you might have done it."

Henry laughed.

"Why?" he said. "Was they scalped?"

"No. Now listen, Henry. Get serious, can't you? Just for a minute? Foster says you had a motive. Everybody seen you have that fight, and Foster thinks that maybe you been holding a grudge against them two since you was the only one got throwed in jail."

"Hell, Charlie. I'd be ashamed to shoot at them white boys. I could whip either one of them with one hand tied, and I reckon if I was a mind to kill them, I'd just get me a good sharp stick."

"I know that," I said, and the funny thing is, I did know it. All of a sudden, I could see how silly I'd been to think that Henry might really be guilty. It was like I had told Foster. Even if Henry had wanted to kill them, he wouldn't have done it the way it had been done.

"I know that, Henry, but Foster's coming out here to talk to you about it in the morning, and I just thought you ought to be ready for him. If you pop off at him like you done in the jail, you'll just likely make him more suspicious of you."

"Talk. Ha."

That was the first sound to come out of old Malachi.

"Papa," said Mose, "they got no evidence against Henry. They going to ask him some questions, that's all. They can't arrest nobody without some kind of evidence."

Malachi studied the dirt floor. Outside an owl hooted. I thought I noticed a slight reaction on Malachi's old face, but I couldn't be sure.

"Our Cherokee courts used evidence," he said. "Now we got no more courts."

Mose rubbed his chin and stared off into the corner of the room. Henry began to get a little nervous and started pacing back and forth across the floor. Old Malachi raised one cheek of his ass to let a fart.

"Henry," I said, "what are you going to do?"

"I don't know," he said. "All I know is, that goddamn Foster ain't going to railroad me for no killings I didn't do. That's for sure."

"Don't do nothing stupid," I said. "At least wait and see what Foster has to say before you do anything stupid. Will you?"

"I think Charlie's right," said Mose.

"Yeah. Yeah," said Henry. "I ain't going to do nothing stupid."

He paced the floor some more, then he stopped, facing the wall. He leaned one hand against one of the logs in the wall and stood there with his back to us.

"I ain't going to do nothing stupid," he said.

"Stupid," said Malachi, and I couldn't tell what he meant by it.

I left them alone a few minutes after that and walked on back home.

CHAPTER TWELVE

It was just a few minutes after we opened up the store the next morning when Foster came in. He had ridden up outside and tied his horse to the hitching rail out in front, so I knew that he was on his way out of town. He went straight to where we kept the boxes of shells and picked up the kind he needed. He always just helped himself to whatever he was after, so all we had to do was to just keep the records straight, which was no small matter in itself, because Foster had two separate accounts with us. He had a personal account on which we recorded clothes and food and stuff like that he bought, and then he had this official account which he used mostly for ammunition and things that he used in his official capacity as a deputy United States marshal. We had to send the statements with his signature on them once a month to Fort Smith, Arkansas, which was the headquarters for the federal law over the Indian Territory, in order to get paid.

"Put these on my tab, will you, George?"

"Sure thing, Ab," said Daddy. "You expecting some trouble this morning?"

"Naw, I ain't looking for no trouble, but you never know in this business. It's best to stay ready for anything that might come up. I've got to ride out to that foreigner's place."

"Frank Motl?"

"Yup. He's going to show me where he found them two boys at, so I can check around the area, you know. Sort of look for any evidence there might be."

He had paused in the middle of his speech while he was putting his name on the bill, and I was just standing there with a lump in my throat, waiting to see what else he might say about what he was planning to do. I didn't have to wait very long.

"Got to stop by the Pathkiller place on the way back into town," he said. "Have a little talk with Henry."

"You think that maybe Henry did those killings?" said Daddy.

"I don't know just yet, George. Henry had a score to settle with them two, though, and I got to question him. So far that's all I got to go on."

He started toward the door, and I hesitated just a second, because I really hated the thought of getting myself into this thing right there in front of Daddy, but when Foster's hand was on the door, I just couldn't let him get out of there. There was too much at stake.

"Mr. Foster," I said. "Wait a minute."

He turned around, and I just stood there.

"Well, what is it, Charlie?" he said.

I didn't know what to say, and when I finally opened my mouth, I just blurted something out before I knew what it was I was saying.

"I went out there last night."

Foster and Daddy were staring at me, and I wished that I had thought up something else to say.

"Where?" said Foster.

Daddy was giving me a real hard look.

"I went out to see Henry," I said. "I told him what happened in here last night, and I told him you were going out there to talk to him this morning."

"You did what?" said Daddy, and the tone of his voice told me that he didn't really want me to repeat what I had just said. He wanted to hear an explanation, but I just ignored him.

"Mr. Foster," I said, "Henry didn't do that shooting. He told me he didn't do it. Besides, it just isn't like him. If Henry wanted to kill someone, he'd do it out in the open. He wouldn't sneak up behind them like that."

"Charlie," said Foster, "I wish you hadn't of done that. Now if Henry is the guilty one, he'll be long gone before I can get out there."

"No," I said. "You don't understand. He didn't do it. He'll be there. I know he will."

"I sure as hell hope you're right. You let one of them full-bloods get out into them hills, you play billy hell trying to run him down."

"Henry'll be at the house, Mr. Foster. That's not what I'm trying to tell you."

"Well, then," said Daddy, "just what are you trying to say, Charlie?"

"Henry, well, Henry thinks you're going to try to pin those killings on him, no matter what. He thinks that you're out to get him and that you're not going to bother with evidence or anything like that."

"Now look here, boy," said Foster. "I'm a lawman. I don't let no personal feelings get in the way of doing my duty, you hear that? I can't help it what he thinks might be in my head. I got a job to do. Two white boys what growed up right here in this town's been murdered, and Henry Pathkiller had a motive for it, and I'm going out there and have a little talk with him. That's all. And he better by God be there."

"Can I ride out there with you, Mr. Foster?"

"What the hell you want to do that for?"

"It's not that I don't trust you, Mr. Foster," I said. "I know that you've got to do your job, and I know that you'll do what's right, but I'm just afraid that Henry's got the wrong idea, and that, well, he might do something foolish when he sees you come riding up out there. Maybe if he sees I'm with you, maybe he'll trust you a little more. That's all."

"I don't see no need for it," said Foster, "and besides that, it seems to me that you've already done too much. I don't know if I'd want to have you riding along behind my back, boy."

Daddy came right out from behind the counter and took several long strides toward Foster. He looked pretty fierce, for Daddy, and for once I was a little proud of him.

"Ab," he said, "I don't necessarily approve of all his friends, and I'll admit that he's got a crazy idea or two in his head, but that's my son. You got no call to go making insinuations like that about my son."

"Aw, hellfire and damnation," said Foster. "All right. All right. Let's just forget the whole son-of-a-bitching thing, all right? I'm sorry I said that about Charlie, George. I take it all back, all right? Charlie, you want to ride along with me, you get a horse saddled and you be down at my office goddamn quick, you hear? I ain't got no more time to waste around here."

"Yes, sir," I said, and my apron was already off over my head. As Foster slammed the door, I heard him say, "Goddamn it to hell." I was right behind him, and as I was going out the door, Daddy was yelling at me.

"I don't know how you expect us to run any kind of business around here," he said.

For once I was really thankful for Daddy's store and for his good name and reputation around town, because I was able to rent me a horse and saddle on credit, and I was in front of Foster's office in almost no time. He came outside and climbed into his saddle.

"Let's go," he said.

He took off like a shot, with me right behind him. After we got out of town, I guess he had cooled down some. He slowed his mount down to a trot, and we rode on out to Mr. Motl's farm. Actually, it was just a rented farm, because nobody owned any land in the Cherokee Nation. The Nation owned all the land, and citizens had the use of it. Any white people in the Cherokee Nation were only just renters, but it looked like things weren't going to stay that way much longer. There was talk of the federal government drawing up a final Cherokee roll and giving us each a private piece of land and opening up the leftover to white people. That was what Henry had been agitating so much over lately. Anyhow, we found Mr. Motl at work on little things that would keep him around the house. He had promised to be there when Foster came. His wagon was already all hitched up, and he drove it out the road with the two of us riding along beside him. We hadn't gone far from his house down the main road when he pulled his wagon up. He climbed down from the seat and walked over to the edge of the road, pointing off and down. The ground sloped away from the road down toward the Illinois River. Between the road and the river was a lot of brush scattered over some very rocky ground. There were also lots of loose rocks, mostly real close together, which must have been the ones

Mr. Motl had been dumping from his wagon in the process of clearing his land.

"It vas here," said Mr. Motl.

"Where exactly, Mr. Motl?" asked Foster.

Mr. Motl walked and slid about halfway down the incline and stopped beside some brush.

"Dey vas here," he said, pointing down into the tangled brush at his feet. "I see from road some bar feets sticking out from dees boosh."

Foster and I followed him down to the spot. There was what looked like bloodstains still there in the dirt. There wasn't much else to see. Foster walked around a little and kicked at some rocks. He took off his derby and wiped his forehead with a sleeve.

"Well," he said, "I guess we might as well be going on our way."

"But, Mr. Foster," I said, "maybe we haven't looked around here enough. Maybe somewhere around here there's something that would tell us something about who did the shooting."

"Do you see anything but dirt and rocks, boy?"

"No, but . . ."

"Mr. Motl, I appreciate your taking your time to lead me out here. You can get on back to work now. Charlie, you can stay here and look at rock all you want. It don't make a damn to me, but I've got other things to do myself."

The two of them climbed back up the slope, and Mr. Motl got back into his wagon. Foster mounted his horse and started back toward town. There didn't seem to be much for me to do but follow him, so I did.

We rode in silence most of the way back toward town, and then we cut off the road in time to go off toward Malachi's cabin. The closer we got to it, the scareder I got. I knew that Henry hadn't shot those two bastards, but I also knew that he didn't trust Foster, and that old Malachi trusted him even less. Or rather, he did trust Foster, and any other white man. He trusted them to always be predictable and do the worst and stupidest thing possible in any given situation. I just hoped that Henry wouldn't do anything foolish. All he had to do was to just talk to Foster—answer a few questions. Foster had no evidence. He couldn't possibly arrest Henry. I wasn't quite sure why I was going along, but I guess that I thought if it looked like Henry was going to try something dumb, well, maybe I would be able to talk him out of it. I

kept hoping the ride up to the cabin would never end, but it did—all
too quickly.

Old Malachi had built his cabin about halfway up on the side of a
hill. The woods were thick all around three sides of the cabin and up on
the hill, but in front of the cabin, going downhill, trees were only
scattered. Foster and I pulled up right at the base of this hill, with all
that open space between us and the cabin. Then we heard a voice cry
out.

"Go back."

That was most often in those hills a warning yelled out to a lawman
by someone who didn't want to kill him but damn sure would if he
failed to heed the warning.

"That son of a bitch," said Foster.

"Hey," I shouted. "Henry. It's Charlie. Foster just wants to ask you a
couple of questions. It's okay, Henry. He even let me ride out here with
him. Come on outside."

"Go back."

I recognized old Malachi's voice that time. Then Mose stepped out
the door, leaving it open.

"Hey, Foster," he called. "You going to take Henry in?"

"I ain't here to take nobody in. Not just yet. I just got some questions for him about them two boys that's killed."

Henry stepped out and kind of pushed Mose aside, stepping around
in front of him. He was holding his rifle.

"Oh God, no," I said, just barely out loud.

"How do I know that, lawman?" yelled Henry.

Foster spoke to me.

"Them bastards is looking for a fight," he said.

"No. Wait a minute," I said. "They're just scared. They think you're
going to take him on in."

Then I shouted up the hill.

"Henry. I wouldn't have come along if there was any tricks. You
ought to know that."

"Hell, Charlie, I trust you, but you don't know what's in that
lawdog's head."

It was real quiet for a minute, and I looked from Foster to Henry and
Mose, expecting all kinds of hell to break loose at any minute and
feeling uneasy and goddamn useless. Henry broke the silence.

"Foster," he said, "you want to talk to me, you get off your horse and come up here. You come up this hill about halfway, and I'll talk to you."

"All right, Henry. I'm coming up."

Foster handed me his horse's reins to hold for him, grabbed the saddle horn with his left hand and the butt of his rifle with his right, and swung his right leg over the top of the horse to dismount at the same time as he pulled the rifle from the saddle boot. Henry quickly jerked his rifle up to his shoulder.

"Not with no rifle," he shouted.

He sent a shot into the ground right between the forelegs of Foster's horse, and both animals, Foster's and mine, started to jump around some. Foster's left foot was still in the stirrup when the shot hit, and he started to hop around trying to get it loose. When he finally did get it loose, he was sent sprawling in the dirt and dropped his rifle. At the same time as Foster was having all that trouble, Mose had run up and grabbed Henry by the arm.

"Henry, don't shoot," he said.

Henry spun around with the butt of his rifle and knocked Mose back against the side of the cabin, where he just sank down to the ground. Henry started running like hell for the trees. Foster scrambled for his rifle, and just as he came up with it and was turning for Henry, there was a ferocious loud yell, like a turkey gobble, and shots started to hit all around us. None of them even came close, but they sure as hell had me scared. Old Malachi had come out the door. He was standing there in front of his cabin with nothing on but his trousers. His mouth was wide open and giving out that yell, and he was holding out in front of him with both hands an old pistol, I think it was a Navy Colt, which I remembered having seen around their house before, but which I thought would never shoot.

"Goddamn son of a bitch," said Foster.

He started working his rifle faster than I had ever seen anyone work a rifle, moving it from the cabin to where Henry was running for the trees. His first shot nearly tore old Malachi's right arm away. The next one hit the dirt between Henry's feet. The next four smashed into Henry's backside, beginning just below the left cheek of his butt and moving in a diagonal line up across his back to his right shoulder. It was all over.

CHAPTER THIRTEEN

I was doing my best to hold the horses still, and when the shooting finally stopped, and I did manage to quiet them down, I could only sit there for a minute stunned. Henry hadn't moved since he'd pitched forward after the last shot tore into his shoulder. I knew that he was dead. Old Malachi was sitting in front of the door of his cabin with his right arm just hanging down at his side looking like something fresh killed. Mose was beginning to stir a little back there against the wall where the blow from Henry's rifle butt had sent him reeling.

"Oh God," I said. "God damn."

"Them crazy bastards started shooting, Charlie," said Foster. "There wasn't nothing else I could do. You seen it."

Mose had come to his senses and was just beginning to take in what all had happened. He looked like he was in shock or something, and he said something to Malachi in Cherokee. The old man answered him the same way. Mose started to walk very slowly toward where Henry was lying all twisted around, and then, without any warning, old Malachi's voice just seemed to swell up and fill the whole goddamn sky, and it was weird, but it was beautiful, too. I didn't really know, but I thought that it was probably some kind of a death song for Henry or a mourning song or something. I didn't know those old songs. Hell, I didn't even know the Baptist Church hymns the way they sang them in Cherokee, but Malachi, he knew everything.

Foster kept standing there with his rifle ready and looking around like he expected thousands of Indians to come pouring out of the woods from all sides at just any time. I got myself down off my rented horse and started to go up the hill to meet Mose. He had stopped right beside the body, and when I got close enough, I could see that his fists were clenched real tight down at his sides, and he looked up through the branches of the trees with a look of disbelief on his face. There were tears running down his cheeks. I wanted to say something to him, but it didn't seem like there was really anything to be said. I looked down at Henry and then up at Mose, and I thought of Annie and of the little baby that had never even had a chance to find out what life was all about. I thought about old Malachi over there behind me all broken. Then Foster was right there beside me, still holding his rifle.

"Mose," he said, "you ain't thinking about carrying this thing no farther, are you?"

Mose didn't answer him. He didn't even look at him. He just dropped slowly to his knees down beside Henry.

"All I wanted was just to question him," said Foster. "He started shooting, and I had to stop him. It's my job. I'm willing to just forget what your old man done and let the whole thing drop right here. Just don't you go getting no foolish notions in your head."

"Mr. Foster," said Mose, real quiet and still not looking up at Foster, "my brother's dead, and my papa's hurt bad. Leave us alone. You done enough around here for one day."

Foster started toward his horse.

"You riding back with me, Charlie?" he asked.

"Mose," I said, "I didn't think—"

Mose interrupted me before I could finish what I wanted to say.

"Charlie," he said, looking right up into my face. That's the only time I can remember him ever looking me right in the face like that, and it sent a cold chill up my spine. Then he went on very quietly.

"Go on back to town," he said.

CHAPTER FOURTEEN

I worked full days at the store for the rest of that week and didn't see anything of Mose or his old man. They didn't come into town or send for a doctor or for an undertaker, so I figured they had buried Henry out in the woods Cherokee-fashion, and they had probably found one of the old Indian doctors out in the hills to take care of Malachi's arm. I just hoped that kind of medicine would be enough for the awful wound he had suffered. I had supper with Velma and her folks again one night that week. Not much of any importance happened anywhere, though. My folks and hers were very careful not to say much about what happened to Henry, and it must have been a terrible strain on them. I knew they all felt like some kind of Divine Providence had taken a hand in earthly affairs to see to it he got what he deserved, and I was reasonably sure that they would have liked to have told me, "I told you so." But I guess to be completely fair to them, I'd have to say that they worked pretty hard at keeping it all to themselves, because they had some concern for my feelings.

On the weekend I had to go out to my cabin again to do some work, or, at least, I had to make it look like that was what I was doing. Everybody except me who had any interest in the affair was getting awfully impatient with my excuses for putting off the wedding. I went out to the cabin, but mostly I just sat around thinking and wishing that I could get up the nerve to go and talk to Mose. I couldn't do it, though. He had sent me away the last time I saw him, and I didn't blame him for it a bit. I didn't know if he would ever want to see me again, and I didn't want to impose myself on him if he didn't—especially after all he had been through. And then there was old Malachi. Even if I had ever managed the courage to go see Mose, I knew that I would never be able to face Malachi again. I had always felt that the old man didn't like me. No, it was even worse than that. I felt like, for some reason, he never found me to be quite worthwhile. It was like I wasn't important enough for him to even dislike.

Well, I messed around with a few things in the cabin, not accomplishing a great deal, and then I'm not sure what it was that I was thinking about doing, maybe going outside and taking a little walk in the woods or something like that, but anyway, I had just turned around there inside my cabin when something scared me so that I jumped clean off the floor and my heart skipped about two beats. What scared me so much was just that I hadn't been expecting anything at all, much less what it was that I saw, because there was Mose standing in the doorway. I hadn't heard him come up or anything, and I don't have any idea how long he had been standing there.

"Hey, I ain't wild," he said.

"Mose," I said, "you nearly scared the shit out of me."

"I thought I'd probably find you out here today."

"Yeah, well, Velma and the folks are all riding me pretty hard these days."

I had never felt quite so awkward with Mose before—I mean, besides when we were there next to Henry's body. But this was just the two of us there together at my cabin, the one that Mose had really done most of the work on, and it was very strange that I didn't have anything to say to him. What was even stranger was that it seemed to matter that I didn't have anything to say. I asked him if he wanted to come in and sit down, and that really sounded stupid. I mean, the place was about as much his as mine. He said that if I didn't mind, he would rather walk out in the woods, so I joined him, and for some time we just walked, neither of us saying anything at all. It seemed a little better like that—the two of us just walking in the woods in silence like there was really no need for us to say anything, because we both knew what was in the other one's heart. Like I say, it made me feel a little better, but I knew that it really wasn't any better at all. Too much had happened for things to ever be the way they had been before, and the realization of that fact made me want to cry. Then Mose started to talk.

"Henry's up the hill behind the old man's house," he said.

I didn't respond. I couldn't think of anything to say. Mose went on.

"The old man," he said, "well, his arm ain't never going to be good for nothing again, but he's alive and mean as ever. I just thought you'd want to know."

"I did, Mose," I said. "I really did. I've been wanting real bad to come out and see you, but I, well, I just didn't know if you'd want me around. I was afraid that . . ."

I started to choke up on my own words, and I had to swallow hard before I could keep talking.

"I was afraid that you might not want nothing more to do with me."

He stopped walking and sat down underneath a tree, leaning back against its trunk.

"Charlie, it ain't your fault," he said. "No more than it's mine. I thought the same as you. I tried to stop him from shooting when I should have been out there with a gun myself. All my life I listened to Henry. I believed everything he ever told me, and he taught me most everything I know. The old man, he just gave up on everything a long time ago, I guess. Mama died, and it begun to look like the Cherokee Nation's dying. Anyhow, he's always been off by himself, inside, I mean, for about as long as I can recall. Henry took care of me. He took real good care of me, too. Taught me to hunt. Taught me to shoot. Fought for me a few times. But he used to tell me, 'Mose,' he'd say, 'you're wasting your time going to that white man's school.' And, 'You're wasting your time working like a white man.' And I'd argue with him. I'd try to tell him, we got to live like white men. We got to learn to make it in their kind of world, or there won't be no world left for us to live in. I'd tell him, 'Henry, you show these white people you got some brains and you ain't lazy, then they'll sit up and take notice of you. There ain't nothing they can do that we can't do, and there ain't nothing to stop us from doing it.' Then Henry'd say, 'There's the United States government, the United States Army, the United States marshals, the United States courts and all them blond, blue-eyed *yonegs* moving into our country like swarms of locusts everywhere you go. That's all there is to stop you.' Charlie, I listened to him about so many different things. The one thing that really mattered, I didn't listen."

We sat there for a little while longer, and then we walked some more. Mose told me that he was moving back into his own cabin, and although I couldn't figure out why he would want to do that when all it could possibly hold for him was bad memories, and, on top of that, old

Malachi probably needed more help than he ever had before, I didn't ask him to explain it to me. He took his leave of me a short while later, and I went back down to my cabin to do some more work, but my heart wasn't in it. I went on home myself.

Sunday morning I went to church with the family and sat with Velma, as usual. After church, we all went over to my folks' house to eat dinner, and then the six of us, me and Velma and both sets of parents, loaded up in a wagon and drove out to the cabin. This had all been prearranged, of course, and I was certain it had been done for the purpose of helping me get things in good shape so as to hurry me on up a little. Oh, sure, they all did kind of just want to see where their children were going to go to live after they got married. Anyway, it was a pretty lousy afternoon, but Daddy and Velma's old man did a lot of work on the place, and I had to, too, just to make the right kind of impression. Velma and our two mamas twittered around something terrible, and I thought that I'd go out of my mind before the afternoon ended. It was all I could manage to do, what with all the work we got done, to keep from being pinned down to a specific date right then and there, but I held them off somehow. Mainly, I just kept acting real ashamed and talking about my small bank account. I guess I was just about beginning to think that I'd be able to carry on like that most indefinitely, but then I had no way of knowing what would happen just about one week later, on that Friday when Harlan Tedford came riding into town.

CHAPTER FIFTEEN

There were a lot of famous lawmen who worked the Indian Territory out of Fort Smith, Arkansas, but Harlan Tedford was about the most famous of the whole lot. He was known as a good lawman, but a mean man. Henry'd have said that there's no difference in the two, and maybe he'd have been right again. Tedford was rumored to have taken in every man he'd ever gone after, most of them dead. And, for some reason, an astonishingly high number of those outlaws had been Chero-kee or Creek Indians. It didn't take long for word to get around that he had ridden into our town just after noon on that Friday and gone into Deputy Foster's office. Foster took him out and bought him a lunch, and then they went back into the office for an hour or so before Foster stuck his head out the door and yelled at Jody Snipes, a lazy kid who just hung out around the streets a lot and happened to be out there at the right time. He gave Jody a nickel and sent him running off down the street. A few minutes later, old Arthur Johnson, Eddie's old man, went into the office, and it wasn't long after that, Jerry Smith's folks showed up. Just like everybody else in town, I was about to go crazy from curiosity, but Daddy said if we just had a little patience, we'd soon find out what was going on, so I did my best to carry on in the store with patience.

Johnson and the Smiths left not long after they had gone into the office, and it wasn't long after that, Harlan Tedford mounted up and rode out again. It was about three in the afternoon when Foster came into the store.

"What can we do for you today, Ab?" said Daddy.

"Aw," said Foster, "I don't want to buy nothing, George. What I really come in here for was to say something to Charlie there."

"Oh well, is it something private?"

"Hell, no, George. Ain't nothing you can't listen in on."

I walked over to where they were standing at the counter near the cash register.

"What is it, Mr. Foster?" I said.

"Charlie, I don't rightly know how to tell you this, but, well, I guess you know that there fellow come into my office was Harlan Tedford. Thing is, it seems that Harlan had been assigned to investigate some kind of mysterious killings that's been going on, mostly over around the old Creek Nation. They was robbery-killings, it seems. Worst one hap-pened near Tulsey. Whole family traveling through in a wagon. They was all killed—man and his wife and four young ones."

Foster stopped for a minute, and I thought I could guess what was coming next.

"Well, Harlan got them. Two men. Scum. He'd got word of what happened here, you know, to them two boys. He brung in some of the stuff he found on them two killers after he'd shot them, to show me—to see if there might be some connection between what happened here and them other killings."

"And there was?" I said.

"Them boys' parents identified their boots, and Jerry Smith's ma recognized a watch she give Jerry on his last birthday. I'm sorry, Charlie. I know what you're thinking, but, Charlie, goddammit, you got to admit that I done my best out there. I didn't want to kill Henry Pathkiller."

"There wasn't any reason," I said, not really to Foster or to anyone. "There just wasn't any reason for it."

"Henry and old Malachi brung it on themselves," said Foster. "They shouldn't have started shooting. Hell, I guess I'll ride out there and at least let them know that Henry weren't no murderer. I guess they'd want to know that, anyway."

"I'm not sure that's going to make a hell of a lot of difference now," I said. "Besides, they know he was innocent."

"All he'd have had to do was to just answer some questions. God damn it to hell."

He was on his way out the door when I called out his name and stopped him.

"What color were they?" I said. "The two men that Tedford got."

"Why, they were white, Charlie. Why?"

"Never mind, Mr. Foster," I said, and he went on out and closed the door.

"There goes a big man," said Daddy.

"What was that?" I said.

"I said he's a big man. It takes that kind to admit a mistake. And when you get right down to it, it wasn't really even his mistake. He was only doing his job, and a thankless job at that. Those Pathkillers, in their ignorance or guilt for God only knows what or something, started to shoot at him and forced him into killing a man. That's a terrible thing to have to do."

I ground my teeth.

"It's Henry that's dead," I said.

"Charlie, you just don't seem to understand."

"Shut up," I yelled. "Just shut up."

I was pulling my apron off over my head as I yelled that to him, and
I couldn't believe my own ears. It was almost like I was somebody else,
and I was standing off to one side watching myself without any control
over what I was doing and without feeling the feelings that must have
gone with it. I hurried to the door and nearly ran over Velma, who was
about to come in. Daddy must have been at least as astonished at what
I had said to him as I was myself, because he never answered at all.
Velma only slowed me down a little bit, just enough for me to go
around her without running right through her, but as I tried to rush on
past and away, she called out to me.

"Charlie," she said. "Charlie, where in the world are you off to in
such a hurry?"

"Velma, please," I said, "just this once, mind your own business, will
you?"

"Charlie? What is it? What is the matter with you?"

"Can't you listen to me for once in your goddamn life, Velma? I just
can't talk now. Not to you or anybody else."

"But I've got to talk to you, Charlie. I've got to. It's very important.
I've come all the way down here just to talk to you, and I can't imagine
what is so almighty important to you that you can't even spare me a
minute when I'm so obviously upset."

"All right," I said, "for God's sake. Will you just shut up for a
minute? I don't want to stand here on the damn street and yell at each
other, okay? Just shut up, and let's get the hell out of here. Let's go
someplace."

"Where? Where do you want to go?"

"Anyplace," I said. "I don't care. Come on."

We started walking, and somehow or other we wound up at the
graveyard. Even in my state of mind, I had to think that it was somehow, in a strange way, funny that we should be there at that particular
time. I don't think that anything would have seemed funny to Velma,
though. The walk had calmed me down some, and I was able to notice
for the first time that she seemed to be genuinely upset about something. I thought at first that it was because of the way I was acting, but
pretty soon I thought that I could tell there was something else that
was really bothering her. She was quiet for a little while, but finally,
when she had taken all she could, she started to talk.

"Charlie," she said, "have you quite gotten ahold of yourself?"

"I don't know, Velma."

"Charlie, I'm serious. Can I talk to you?"

"Yeah," I said. "Go ahead. I guess I can listen to just about anything anymore."

"I don't know what's the matter with you, Charlie, but we are in serious trouble, unless you're prepared to take some action. You've got to help me, Charlie."

I could imagine all kinds of nagging about to come up about how Mama and Daddy were wondering if I was ever going to get serious and all that stuff that I'd heard a hundred times before, and there was nothing that I wanted to listen to less right at that time.

"Velma, for God's sake," I said, "what's wrong with you?"

"I'm pregnant, Charlie. I'm going to have a baby."

I started to laugh. I know it was an awful thing to do, but I couldn't help myself, and I just rolled back on old Granny Hotchkiss and held my sides and laughed. When I finally got myself pulled back together, Velma was practically hysterical. She was crying and shaking all over, but I talked to her and got her calmed down some. I told her to go on back home and to tell her mama that I had finally come across and popped the old question. I told her to ask her mama to go ahead and make all the proper arrangements and to set everything up for as soon as possible, and we'd get married. Well, that seemed to be all she really cared about. She got real happy again all of a sudden and threw her arms around me and started to kiss me right there in broad daylight. She finally quit and hurried home to make all the plans, and I got up and started to walk out to see Mose.

CHAPTER SIXTEEN

There was no one real important reason for my going out to see Mose that afternoon. I wanted to tell him about Henry, and I wanted to tell him about my latest problem. It wasn't really a new problem. It just made the old ever-present one more pressing. And as far as the news about Henry was concerned, Mose and Malachi and me had all known the truth all along. What Foster had said wouldn't make much difference. I suppose the main reason I wanted to see Mose was simply the mood I was in. I needed someone to talk to—to really talk to—and there just wasn't anybody except Mose who would do. There had been several years of my life passed since I had realized that was one of the facts of existence for me. Well, there had been Henry. I could usually talk to Henry, but Henry was older, and there were some things that I couldn't talk to Henry about. Besides that, Henry was gone, and there was only Mose.

By the time I got out to Mose's cabin, I was pretty much over the strange mood that had come over me at the store. In fact, I was beginning to feel a little bit ashamed of the way I had yelled at Daddy and at Velma, but not really very much. Mainly, I was very surprised at myself and just kept going over and over what I had said and done. The more I rehashed it in my mind, the less ashamed I felt, and I finally was kind of enjoying it, still like I had only watched it, though, like someone else had really done all that stuff.

I found Mose at the cabin, and I told him the whole thing. I told him about Foster and Harlan Tedford and the two white men who were the real killers. He didn't say anything, but he just looked out through the window into the trees. Then I told him how I had blown up at Daddy, and how Velma had showed up just then, and I'd laid into her, too. He laughed a little at that. He said that I had needed to do that for a long time, and I agreed with him. Then I told him about Velma's news and how I was really and truly going to have to get hitched up to her, but I was going to move with her out to my cabin and be his neighbor, so it wasn't all bad. He tried to show some pleasure at that news, but I could tell that he wasn't really too thrilled about it. I think Mose had known long before me that I would never be happy with Velma. He got up and pulled a jug of moonshine off a shelf on the wall. He uncorked it and took a long drink, then he handed the jug to me. I took a drink from it and handed it back to Mose. As I did, I looked up him, and I thought just then that he looked so much older than he should. Me and him were just the same age, but he looked so much older. He was like Henry all of a sudden, or maybe even older than that.

"Let's take one last walk in the woods, Charlie," he said.

I got up and followed him outside, wondering why he had said that it was to be a last walk, but I didn't ask him. I just followed him along. He carried that jug with him, and now and then he'd tip it up and take a swallow and then pass it back to me. The woods were beautiful. It was springtime, and everything was new green. You could smell wild onions and listen to the red squirrels fussing with each other. I thought that I'd like to just keep walking deeper and deeper into the dark woods until I had left all my troubles behind me. I imagined that there was a whole other world way in there somewhere that me and Mose could go to and no one would ever see us again. The whiskey made me light-headed and made the fantasy even more easy to believe. I got to thinking that I could hardly wait until we got there, and I also got to thinking that Henry would be there waiting for us and laughing at how stupid we'd been, moping around out here and thinking that he was dead and all. I remember stumbling a time or two, and I remember Mose giving me a hand and talking to me, but I can't remember anything that he said. I guess that I got pretty drunk, because I don't remember how I got there, but the next thing I remember is I woke up and it was morning. I was on the dirt floor of Mose's cabin, and Mose was already up and had some coffee made. He poured me out a cup and put it on the table.

"How's your head, Charlie?" he said.

"It ain't too bad, Mose," I said. "I'll be all right after I drink that coffee there."

Mose made real good coffee. I always liked it the way he made it better than I liked anybody else's coffee—even Mama's. We drank a couple of cups, and then Mose cooked up some potatoes and some bacon, and we ate breakfast. Mose cleared off the table, and he gave me another cup of coffee. Then he walked across the room and picked up his rifle.

"Charlie," he said, "I was going hunting today. You feel like doing some hunting?"

He was standing by the window loading some shells into his hunting rifle. I was still sitting at the table, slurping on my last cup of coffee.

"Sure thing, Mose," I said. "I'm always ready."

It was just at that time that we heard the horse coming up to the cabin. That damn fool Foster had made his last ride.

CHAPTER SEVENTEEN

I don't know how or why Foster had wound up at Mose's place. Maybe he had gone over to talk to Malachi, and the old man wouldn't have anything to do with him, so he had gone looking for Mose. Maybe he had never known that Mose had moved back in with the old man temporarily after Annie died and had gone looking for Mose first. I don't know, and somehow it doesn't seem to make much difference now, anyhow.

That was how it happened that I was out there that day when Mose killed a deputy United States marshal, and how I came to be out there in the hills with him afterward. I guessed that Mose had just decided to sort of declare war—a private war—on the whites who had driven his people west, who had then taken their Nation away from them after they had been out west for a while and had really built it up, and who had finally refused him and his people a decent place in their own country. Then, to punctuate the whole thing, they had killed his brother and shot up his old man. After he came to the realization that Henry had been right all along, I guess that he had just decided to put his own finish on the whole mess, but I wanted to find out from him, so I asked him.

"Mose, what are we going to do now?" I said.

"Get some sleep, Charlie."

"No, I mean from now on. You know."

"What you do is up to you, Charlie. I ain't going to try to tell you what to do."

"Well, I want to stay with you, Mose, but do you know what you're going to do?"

"I'm going to take and kill me some more lawdogs."

"What for, Mose? I mean, Foster was the one who shot Henry. Why you want to kill some more of them?"

"Well, for one thing, Charlie, I ain't really got much choice in it no more. I done killed one of them. They're going to send more of them out to get me, and when they do, I'm going to kill them."

I didn't answer him. He looked over at me, and he was kind of smiling.

"They're going to get me, I reckon," he said. "Sooner or later. All I can do is my best to make it as much later as I can."

"I'm sorry that it had to turn out like this," I said.

"Are you talking about history, Charlie? If you're talking about history, I am, too. But if you're talking about me and Foster and what's happening now, it didn't just turn out."

"What do you mean, Mose?"

"Charlie," he said, "when I seen that son of a bitch ride up to my house, I knew if I shot him that I'd have to go on killing them until they get me. I thought before I shot, Charlie. Henry taught me that. If that makes a difference to you, well, you can still find your way home. It's okay if you want to go."

"It don't make no difference to me, Mose," I said. "I guess I really knew it all along."

We slept out under the trees that night, and the next day we just kept going on deeper into the woods. About midafternoon we came up on the old cabin where Annie had grown up. The old folks had both died sometime back, and of course Annie was gone, so Sarah was living there all by herself. We went in to see her, and we just chatted for a bit before Mose let her know what was going on—that the two of us weren't just out hunting again. I don't know just when or how she had found out about it, but she already knew that Henry had been killed by Abner Foster, and she seemed real pleased to find out that Mose had killed Foster. Then somehow I got the feeling that Mose and Sarah wanted to be alone. I began to feel like I was in the way, so I made some kind of excuse, and I left the cabin. I went out a ways, and I lay down under a big tree to wait, and it made me think of when Mose and me were just kids and had to wait for Henry when he was visiting Sarah. Only that had never bothered me the way this did. After a while, Mose came out of the house and found me.

"You ready to go, Charlie?" he said.

"Yeah. I reckon."

I guess he could tell that something was wrong with me from the way my voice sounded.

"What's the matter?" he said. "You beginning to think maybe you should have stayed at home? This is as far out as you've ever been, ain't it?"

"Aw, hell," I said, "it ain't that, Mose."

"What is it then?"

He kind of cocked his head and looked at me, then he turned around and walked a few steps away from me. He stopped and turned to face me again.

"You're thinking about Annie, ain't you? You're thinking that what I just done in there ain't right."

"Mose, it ain't none of my business."

He sat down in the grass facing me.

"Charlie, in the old Cherokee way, when a man's wife died, he might marry her sister, and if a woman lost her husband, she might marry her husband's brother. I guess it's because that's the closest they could come to their lost loved ones. You don't know about that, because that ain't the way you was brought up. It ain't nothing against the dead, Charlie. It's just that life has to go on. Me and Sarah, we can love each other, and we can love Annie and Henry at the same time. In the old days, a man might even marry both sisters at the same time, or a woman might marry both brothers. It happened. That other way, the way you was taught, that's the white man's way."

He was quiet for a while after that. Maybe he was waiting for me to offer some kind of response, or maybe he was just thinking. I don't know, but finally I did answer him.

"Mose?"

"Yeah, Charlie?"

"I didn't know that," I said. "I never heard that before, but it makes sense. I'm glad you told me."

He reached over and slapped me on the back of the shoulder.

"Hey," he said. "Let's get a move on."

We went farther on into the woods—farther than I'd ever been before—before we stopped that night, and we slept out under the trees again. I wondered what my folks and Velma were thinking. They probably thought that after my temper fit, I had just gone out to the cabin to do some work and was still out there. That's what they would think, unless one of them had gone out there to see me for some reason or other. I wondered how long it would take before somebody found Foster out there in front of Mose's house. He nearly always made a point of telling somebody in town where he was going, and he was bound to have been missed by then.

As I lay down under the trees that Sunday night, I thought about what would probably happen in town the next morning. Nobody would worry about me much until then, but when Daddy and Mama got up and found out that I wasn't there on a Monday morning ready to go to work as usual, then they'd know that I didn't just go out to the cabin to pout for a weekend. Probably Foster's body would have been found by then, and it was bound to occur to them that I might be with Mose, wherever he was. Then I thought of something else, and it made me laugh out loud. Mose rolled over on his side and looked at me.

"What's so funny?" he said.

"I was just thinking about Velma," I said. "I bet when she finds out that I ain't in town, she's going to think that I run off to get out of the wedding."

I was still laughing at the thought when Mose asked me another question.

"Did you, Charlie?"

I stopped laughing and thought about it for a minute.

"I don't know, Mose. Goddamn. Now that I think about it, I really don't know."

CHAPTER EIGHTEEN

Instantly, the Red Selagwutsi *strike you in the very center of your Soul—instantly.* Yu.

Mose and I had been out in the hills just a little over a week. We did a little hunting, but Mose was concerned about saving his ammunition, so we set traps to catch squirrels and such, and we fished some. Once we even got a mess of crawdads with a piece of fresh-killed rabbit for bait. Occasionally we would come across an isolated cabin out in the woods. Actually, I guess that Mose knew where they were all the time and that he went to them on purpose, but anyway, we would always get a free meal from the full-bloods that lived in them. I didn't get to know any of these people. They didn't speak any English, and I didn't know enough Cherokee to more than catch a word here and there, but once Mose explained to them that I was all right and was with him, they welcomed me into their homes and fed me. They were the only people we had seen the whole time since Mose had shot Foster. Both of us knew, though, that someone was bound to be out looking for us, or at least for him, by that time. They had to have found Foster and to have figured Mose for the killer, and when a deputy marshal got killed, they were very quick about going after the one who had done it. We hadn't said anything to each other about it, but I think both of us knew, and both of us knew that the other one knew. I did notice that Mose had started watching over his shoulder and looking back down our trail a lot more the last few days.

Then one day we were going through some trees when we came across a cabin. It wasn't really a cabin, just some old skinny trees kind of stacked up on each other to form a front for where a cave, shallow and probably at least partially handmade, was formed in the side of a hill. There were branches thrown over the top to make a roof.

"We'll go in here," Mose said.

Then he stopped and called out.

"Shalleloski."

An old man appeared at the door.

" *'Siyo,* " said Mose.

" *'Siyo. Tohigwus?* " the old man replied.

"Tohigwu," said Mose. *"Nihina?"*

Then the old man looked at me real hard. Mose continued talking to him in Cherokee. The old man answered him and went inside.

"Come on," Mose said to me, and we followed the old man into his house. Inside there were rattles made from turtle shells and gourds. There was a buck's head and antlers hanging on the wall. It wasn't mounted there the way it would be in a white man's house. It was really just the skin from the head fixed so that a man could wear it like a mask. There was more strange stuff around the place, but I can't remember just what it all was. The old man brought us some food. Nobody said anything until we had finished eating, but in the meantime I had a good chance to look the old man over. He must have been just about my size, sort of medium, I guess, but his old body was beginning to sag some with age. He had on a pair of old brogans and overalls, but no shirt, and he had a very remarkable face. It was intense somehow, and round and full, but in spite of that and the full head of straight black hair, I could tell that he was very old. When we had finished eating, he and Mose said a few more things to each other. Then Mose turned to me.

"Old Shalleloski is a doctor," he said. "He's the one that fixed up Papa's arm for us. He's just been telling me that we're apt to have us some visitors out here before long."

"Oh yeah," I said. "Who's that?"

"Four lawmen riding on our trail. Some of the people out here been watching them on the trail for a couple of days."

Then Mose said some more stuff to the old man in Cherokee, ending with *"Ge ga,"* which I knew meant that we were leaving, and we got up without wasting any more time and left. Mose was moving pretty fast, like he knew exactly where he was going.

"Mose," I said, "you think we can lose them?"

"Why try, Charlie?"

I didn't try to answer that. I concentrated on keeping up with him, as he headed up a pretty steep and rocky hill. We got up to the top, and Mose paused for a few seconds.

"You wait here, Charlie," he said.

He took off running along the top of that hill, and when he disappeared into the trees, I sat down on a rock to wait. I had no idea what he was up to, and I started to get worried when, after what seemed to me about an hour and a half had passed, there was no sign of Mose anywhere. It was almost sundown when he did come back and came walking up to me.

"They ought to be here about breakfast time," he said.

"You seen them?"

"Yeah, I seen them. There's four of them all right."

He started to walk back toward where the trees were thicker, and I followed. He stopped at a shaded and grassy spot and lay down on the ground.

"Better try to get some sleep, Charlie," he said. "We're going to be up early in the morning."

Well, I tried. I tried like hell, but just thinking about those four men on their way after us was a little too much for me. I wondered how far away they were and what would happen when they did get to where we were. And I wondered who they were. Then it came into my head that maybe they weren't after me at all. Maybe they didn't know that I was with Mose, and maybe I could get up right that minute and get the hell out of there before it was too late. Then I looked over to where Mose was already asleep and wished that I could be that calm, and I got kind of ashamed of myself for what I had been thinking. I don't know how long it took for me to finally fall asleep, but I was still sound asleep when, the next thing I knew, Mose was kicking at my foot to wake me up, and it was morning.

"Hey, Charlie."

"Oh yeah," I muttered, rubbing my eyes. Then, suddenly remembering where we were and what we were expecting, I jumped to my feet.

"Where are they?" I said.

"Relax, Charlie. I been keeping an eye on them old boys. You got time for a cup of coffee. Here."

I took the coffee he offered me and set it down in the grass where I
had been sleeping. I was looking off in the distance to see if I could spy
anyone coming. Mose kept talking.

"I'd have let you sleep on," he said, "you looked so snug, like a baby,
but I didn't want you to have to wake up to gunshots a little later."

"Where are they, Mose? How close are they?"

"Drink your coffee, Charlie. They'll be here in a little while."

"Goddamn, Mose," I said, "you got a fire going. They'll see the
smoke."

I jumped up again and was about to stomp on the fire, but Mose
took hold of me by the shoulders, not rough, just real firm.

"Charlie," he said, "get ahold of yourself, will you? They see that
smoke, it'll just save us all a little time. I know what I'm doing. Drink
your coffee."

I sat down and drank my coffee. Mose poured himself a second cup.
We didn't talk anymore for a while. Then, when Mose had finished his
second cup, he ran over to the rocks where I had waited for him the
night before. Pretty quick, he ran back to me at the fire.

"You got about time for one more cup, Charlie," he said.

"No, thanks."

He picked up his rifle and started back for the rocks again.

"*Inena,*" he said. "Come on."

I grabbed my rifle and followed him to the rocks. I didn't know why
I wanted the rifle. I sure didn't feel like I would be able to use it. When
we got to the spot Mose had picked out, I looked out over the edge of
the rocks and I could see why he had situated us there. We were up on
the edge of some high hills that ran along one side of a long and deep
valley, and we could see for miles in either direction down in the valley.
Then I saw the four riders. They weren't yet close enough for me to tell
anything more about them than that. They were four riders. But I
didn't take my eyes off them until they got that close. Then my head
started to pound real hard.

"Mose," I said, "that's Harlan Tedford."

"Yeah?"

His expression didn't change at all, except his one eyebrow raised up
a little.

"Which one, Charlie?"

"On the black horse. Riding out front just a bit."

"*Osda,*" he said. "Good." And he raised his rifle to his shoulder and took aim and just held it there while the four lawmen rode closer. Then I saw his finger begin to tighten on the trigger, and he started to kind of sing, very low, so that even I could barely make out what he was saying from my spot right there beside him. I can remember it, because it was what Henry used to say as he took aim at an animal when we were out hunting.

"Usinaliyu Selagwutsi Gigagei getsuhneliga tsudandagihi ayeliyu, usinuliyu. Yu."

I looked back down in the valley again just in time to see Tedford's horse jerk and fall as the shot echoed in the hills simultaneously with the last syllable out of Mose's mouth. Tedford came up fast from under his horse and headed for some nearby rocks, dragging one leg, but he never made it. Mose's second shot caught him right in the middle and doubled him up not far from the horse. Two of the others were headed for the same rocks, one riding hard, the other running on foot, having dismounted at the first shot. The last one was just trying to hold his horse still with one hand while he pulled his rifle out of its boot with the other hand, and he was looking up in our general direction like a damn fool. Mose picked the one on his feet who was getting close to the big rocks as his second target, and he got him in the back just in time, sending him sprawling across the rock that he had likely chosen as his protection. Just about then, the last two, who were both still on horseback, turned their horses almost together and lit out in the direction they had come from. Mose stood up in plain sight to squeeze off just one more round, which caught the slower of the two in the right shoulder and nearly knocked him out of the saddle. He managed to keep his seat, though, and as the two of them rode on out of sight, Mose raised his rifle above his head and shouted after them at the top of his voice.

"I'm Mose Pathkiller," he yelled. "Pathkiller."

Then he let out a loud yell, like a turkey gobble, like I had heard old Malachi give out with that time before, and it looked like it had the same effect as goosing those two horses in the ass, causing them to move even faster. They didn't slow down as long as we were able to see them, and when they were completely out of sight, we went on down into the valley to get the guns and ammunition off the bodies.

CHAPTER NINETEEN

Mose said there was really no reason for us to run any farther back in the hills just yet. He said that as soon as those two got back to civilization and reported what had happened, there would be some more come out there. Four hadn't been enough. They would send six, maybe seven men, he said, and they would probably come with a wagon to use for hauling the two bodies back in for burial. They would be expecting us to have run off again, and probably the plan would be to drop off a couple of men to do the hauling, while the rest of them set about trying to pick up our trail. They would never think of looking for a second ambush in the same spot, so that was just what we were going to give them. Then we would move back in the hills some more.

The next time, though, he wanted to be closer to them. He no longer needed anyone to get away to carry the news back to others, and he wanted to kill them all, if possible. We crossed to the other side of the valley to a spot about halfway up the hill from the rocks that Tedford and the other deputy had tried to reach for cover. We worked the best part of the next day digging out an open place in the side of the hill and walling it off in front with rocks so that we had a small fortress. We fixed a place right in the center of the wall on the inside to stash our ammunition and extra guns. Then, just to be prepared for any event, we cleared ourselves a path on up to the top of the hill and placed rocks along it for protection. We tried it out a few times to see if we could run from our little fortress to the top with comparative ease, and Mose had me run it once by myself while he watched from down below in the valley to see if he could have gotten off a clean shot at me. Toward the end of our second day of work on the hillside, when we had just about completed it, Mose said that we should go back and visit old Shalleloski again. After he ran back up on the hill and along it once more to check out the valley for any riders that might be coming, we went back to the old man's house. He greeted us as before, but without his previous suspicion of me. He fed us as before. Then he and Mose talked, and I waited in silence. Mose took our leave for us, and we left.

"Word is," he told me, as we were walking back to our rock pile, "that I raised quite a fuss. There's already a new pack of lawdogs gathering in Tahlequah to come out here after me, and after them bodies, just like I figured. They ought to be here in three, four days."

"Did he know how many?"

"Naw. They're just all running around now, still trying to get organized. They ain't left yet. It won't be long, though."

"Nothing about me?" I asked.

"Nope," said Mose. "It appears like they don't know nothing about you, Charlie."

I should have been relieved at that news, but I wondered why nobody had connected the fact that I was missing to Mose killing those lawmen. I also began to wish that I had killed me one or two of them. When Mose had been shooting at them, all I could do was watch, fascinated, and a little bit horrified. And when we had gone down to the bodies to get the guns and stuff, I was almost sick. But now I wished that I had got me at least one of them. I really did. I wanted them to know that I was out there, too. I wanted the law to go looking for Mose Pathkiller and Charlie Blackbird, and I wanted them to be saying back in town that Mose and Charlie had killed some more deputies. I especially wanted Velma and Daddy to know. Velma. Damn, I thought. Why the hell did I have to start thinking of her? I wondered if her old lady had set a date for the wedding, and if so, when it was set for. Had I already missed it? I hoped so, just a little, but then I kind of felt sorry for Velma—to be stood up on her wedding day and her getting bigger and bigger every day.

"Hey, Mose?"

"Yeah, Charlie."

"How long does it take a girl, when she's pregnant, you know, how long does it take before you can see her belly starting to get big?"

"Different times for different women, Charlie. Some of them, you can't hardly never tell. Others real soon."

"Well, how soon is real soon?"

"Oh, about at least three months, I'd say, Charlie."

"That long?"

"Yeah, Charlie. That long at least. Most a lot longer than that."

I had been imagining that Velma was just going to sort of blow up all of a sudden, and I guess that I was a little disappointed that she probably didn't look any different at all right at that very moment. And then, what I really didn't expect at all to happen to me, I started to think that I really missed old Velma. Oh, I didn't really miss Velma, I mean, not like you really miss someone. I didn't want to talk to her, and I sure as hell didn't want to listen to her. I did kind of want to see her, but not nearly as much since Mose had told me that she wouldn't be fat yet. I kind of wanted to see her fat. I guess that I wanted to see what I had done. But what I really missed was how often I used to be able to make love to her. I guessed that was all. But I really did miss that.

We walked on back to our fortress, where we spent the major part of the next three days and nights. It was getting to the point where that rock pile seemed almost like home. About the middle of the third night, it started to rain.

CHAPTER TWENTY

When the rain started coming down, Mose and I left our barricade and headed for the shelter of some trees up on the top of the hill. Neither one of us was able to get back to sleep just then, but I lay down under a tree and tried to rest and stay dry. Mose wandered off somewhere. When daylight came it was still raining, and Mose was still gone. I couldn't get a fire started for coffee, so I just got out my bundle, which still had some of the dried meat we had brought along with us right at the beginning. We had saved it as much as we could, kind of for emergencies when we couldn't find anything else to fill our bellies with. I was gnawing on it when Mose came back. He was a little in a hurry.

"They're on the way, Charlie," he said. "We got to get on down there behind that wall before they get close enough to see anything."

We went down the hill and crawled in behind our wall. We had to lie down practically all the way to keep out of sight, but each of us had a little nook in the rocks we could look out of down onto the place where the bodies were.

"Charlie," Mose said, "you don't need to do nothing but just lay here out of sight and keep quiet until I start shooting."

"How many of them are they, Mose?" I asked.

"I seen nine. Two of them in a wagon and seven on horseback."

"I'm going to help you," I said.

"You don't have to do that."

"I'm going to."

"Just wait for my move."

"Okay."

The rain was coming down hard as ever, and I thought that the laws would never get there. Finally, even through the rain, I heard the noise of the wagon and the horses sloshing through the mud. Then I heard some voices, but I couldn't make out what they were saying. I turned my head a little to get a look out through my nook in the rocks, and I thought that I was looking at the whole goddamned United States Army. They had spotted the bodies, which wasn't hard to do, since one of them was Tedford's horse, and they had pulled up right below where we were hidden. Some of them were looking around up at the hills, and for a minute I thought that they suspected that we were up there, but then I got the idea that they were only speculating on where the shots that had killed the two deputies and the horse had come from, and I breathed a sigh of relief. I noticed that they were all wearing their slickers, which I figured would make it a little harder for them to get to their weapons, at least, to their pistols, when the shooting started. Two of the men went around to the rear of the wagon and let down the tailgate. Four others had gone to pick up the two bodies. With four of them having their hands full, struggling to make their way through the mud to the rear of the wagon, Mose decided it was time to go into action.

"Now," he said, and he sat straight up behind the wall and got off three shots almost before I was able to react to his voice. I was up right beside him, though, and I saw three men fall in the mud. The rest of them were scattering in all different directions. I realized that I was just sitting there with my rifle in position, but I hadn't fired a shot. I couldn't. The four men who had been carrying the bodies just dropped them when they heard the first shot, and three of them dove under the wagon. The fourth one jumped into the wagon. I guess that he thought the sides would give him good cover, and maybe he didn't realize how far up above him the shots were coming from. Anyway, it was the worst place he could have gone. He was in plain sight from where we were, and he had rolled over on his back trying to reach under his slicker to get a pistol, while looking up the side of the hill to see if he could find out where we were. Mose put a shot right into his belly. There was a slight pause in the fireworks.

Mose dropped back down, and then he reached up with one hand and pulled me after him.

"Charlie," he said, "just stay down, will you?"

I started to get tears in my eyes, and then I was glad it was raining so hard. Maybe Mose would never notice them. He was peering out from between the rocks again.

"Three under the wagon," he said, "and two right down here in the rocks."

I turned around so I could see again, too, brushing my eyes as well as I could when I turned. Mose sat up again, this time without any warning to me, and pumped five shots right into the bed of that damn wagon. He must have gotten somebody under there, but we couldn't tell right then, and anyway, that must have been what they were waiting for. The two behind the rocks just under us started shooting, and someone started shooting from behind the wagon. He must have crawled through to the side opposite us while we were back down behind the wall. The other two must have still been under the wagon— maybe hit. Mose dropped down again.

"I think three left, Charlie," he said.

I didn't say anything. I was afraid of what my voice might sound like if I tried.

I was beginning to wonder how much longer we would be there, everybody afraid to raise his head, when I noticed through my rocks one of the two men below jump up and start to run. I guess that he was going for a better position, but Mose had seen him too, and he was up again quick and sent a bullet into the man, who looked like he just

decided to take a forward roll. The last two tried to take advantage of
Mose's temporary abandonment of his cover, and they both exposed
themselves to open fire at him. With the two of them up, I decided
that I could once more try my hand, and I sat up beside Mose just as a
bullet smashed into the wall right beside me, sending a sharp piece of
rock into my side. I grabbed my side and slumped forward over the top
of the wall. Mose must have thought that I had been shot, but he
squeezed off one more round, which laid out the one down the hill,
before he reached over to pull me back down below the wall. As he
tried to pull my dead weight back, he must have thrown his own weight
too much against the rocks, because they gave way, and he started to
slide, upside-down, down the slick side of the hill. The deputy behind
the wagon must have thought I was done for, because when he saw
Mose in that shape, he very calmly stepped out from behind the
wagon, taking careful aim. It was a good thing I didn't have time to
think, otherwise I might never have done it, but when I saw him
drawing a bead on Mose, I pulled myself straight up raising my rifle,
and I blew the top of the deputy's head off.

CHAPTER TWENTY-ONE

Mose managed to get himself to his feet, but he was still sliding, and as
he tried to pull his rifle up into position to defend himself against the
one lawman he knew was left, his feet went out from under him, and
he sat down hard on his ass. He raised the rifle fast. Then he just sat
there. He looked at the deputy with part of his head missing, and then
he looked up to where I was still sitting behind our rock wall. Mose
looked like he was every bit as astonished at what I had done as I was.

The only possible danger left was from the two who were still underneath the wagon, and Mose went cautiously the rest of the way down
the hill and over to the wagon. He must have seen that they were dead,

because he came right back up to me as fast as he could make it uphill in the mud.

"Charlie," he said. "Charlie. You hit bad?"

"Naw," I said, "it hurts like hell right now, but it ain't bad. I ain't even really hit. Just a piece of rock."

I showed him where the bullet had hit the rock and chipped it.

We gathered up our supplies and took off. I didn't have any idea where we were going anymore, and I think that even if I had tried, I couldn't have found my way back home. The rain was still coming down as much as ever, and it kept up all the rest of the day. We didn't get a chance to try to catch us anything to eat, and if we had, we wouldn't have been able to get a fire going to cook it, so when it just got to be too much for us, we ate parched corn as we traveled. I stayed hungry the whole time, though. My side was throbbing, and I felt weak from hunger. I think that the rain had begun to get to me, too. I had been out in it most of the night and all of that day, and I was starting to sniff, and my head was all messed up. Mose got way ahead of me a couple of times and had to come back for me. Then he realized that I was moving a lot slower than usual, and he slowed down to stay with me. For the first time since he had killed Foster, I was slowing him down. Late in the afternoon, Mose found some real thick trees that gave a little shelter, and we went in under them. He told me to lie down and rest, and then he went to work cutting and dragging branches which he tangled together to keep the rain all the way off us. There was nothing dry around, though, which he could start a fire with, and the ground was already soaked. I must have gone almost straight to sleep in spite of all the discomfort, because the next thing I remember it was morning, and Mose was very gently shaking my shoulder to wake me up.

"Charlie? Charlie?"

I moaned a little and opened my eyes. I was all curled up in a ball, and I was lying on my hurt side.

"How you feeling this morning, Charlie?"

"I think I'm sick, Mose," I said, and my voice was little more than a whisper. "I'm sick."

He rolled me over on my back, and when I moved I got a sharp pain in my side, and I cried out a little. Mose looked down at where I'd been hit.

"Charlie," he said, "there's blood on your shirt."

He pulled my shirttail out of my trousers and looked at the wound. "You damn fool, Charlie," he said. "You should have told me about this."

"It ain't that, Mose," I moaned. "I'm sick. I just got a damn cold or something from the damn rain. I ain't hurt."

He grabbed my head and pulled it up off the ground and turned it so that I could look down at my own side.

"You ain't, huh? It ain't that, ain't it?"

I had an awful gash along my side where the sharp piece of rock had slashed into it, and it was beginning to look kind of gooey with pus, and my skin was black all around the cut. I only thought that I felt sick before I looked at that, then I suddenly felt like I wanted to puke, but there was nothing in my stomach. Mose had put my head back down and was gathering our stuff.

"Goddamn," he said. "You should have told me, Charlie. We got to get you someplace."

He helped me up off the ground, but I could hardly even stand by myself, so he had me put an arm around his shoulder, and he held me up as we walked through the rain. It seemed to me that we would never get anywhere, that for the rest of my life I would be hanging on to Mose, trying to hold myself up but unable to do so without his help. There would always be the hills and the woods and that empty gnawing pain in my stomach, which kind of moved through my body to center itself with all its intensity in my right side. And there would always be the rain. Then all of those things just became mixed together in a great swirl. Trees and mud and rain and pain were spinning around me, and there was no up or down. The only stable thing in the whole world was Mose, and if I let go of him, I knew that I would be lost in that swirl.

After the spinning started, I remember things only as from a dream, only in bits and pieces from here and there. There was Mose holding me together.

"Just hang on, Charlie. We going to get there," he was saying.

There was thunder and lightning. Then there was Velma with the hugest belly I've ever seen on anything in my whole life, and it just kept getting bigger and bigger until it finally kind of exploded, and when the light from the flash died down, there was old Shalleloski looking into my face with antlers growing out of his head. I knew that I had become warm and dry somehow, and I could see figures moving around me and hear voices, but I could only understand little bits of what they were saying, just something here and there.

"*Skwali,*" said the old man's voice.

"Drink it, Charlie. It's like a tea," Mose was saying. "It'll help fix you up."

A thick, hot liquid was pouring down my throat and running down my chin.

"*Sge. Galunlati hinehi hinehiyu hinidawe, utsinawa aduhniga.*"

Then I thought that I was swimming in that black, smelly stuff.

"*Skwali.*"

"Listen."

"Relief has come."

"*Hinehi hinehiyu hinidawe.*"

"Forever you dwell. Forever you dwell. Relief has come."

"Drink."

"*Skwali.*"

"Drink."

Then the old man was gone, but Mose was still there. Mose would always be there. And we were going again. Again there were the hills and trees, and again the rain. The great god water. Once I felt that we were sliding in the mud—*skwali*—and I thought that I saw the deputy with the top of his head gone, standing at the foot of the hill beside the wagon, waiting for us to slide down to his feet so he could kill us. Then I was lying down again, but on something solid this time, like boards. Then there was a sudden lurch, and I was moving again. Still in the rain. I looked up once, and there was Mose, but now he had his back to me. The moving seemed endless, just like the walking, but it did end, and I felt myself being lifted up and carried somewhere. There was nothing to see but the darkness. Then I was lying down again, and Mose was talking to me.

"I'm sorry, Charlie. It was the only way. You going to be okay now."

Then there was a pounding, and then the noise of a wagon pulling away real fast, and everything was dark again.

"Relief has come."

The only thing that I noticed for a while after I woke up again was that I was warm and dry and still. Then I realized that I was in my own bed, and there was my old lady sitting there beside the bed, looking into my face, and when she saw that I was looking back, she got all excited.

"Charlie?" she said. "Charlie?"

"Mama?"

"George," she called out. "George, he's awake."

Daddy came hurrying into the room.

"Thank God," he said. "How do you feel, son?"

"I don't know," I said. "Warm and dry and still. Where . . . ?"

"It's all right, son," said Daddy. "You just rest and get your strength back. We'll talk later. Your mama and me, we just thank God you're all right. You rest up now."

CHAPTER TWENTY-TWO

It was the next day before the folks decided that it was all right to talk to me about what had happened. The doctor had been called to see me and had cleaned up and dressed the gash on my side. He had left me some medicine, and Mama saw to it that I took it when I was supposed to. I still felt weak, and my side still hurt, but all in all I was feeling much better already. That day they both came into my room together and sat down at my bedside. They seemed just a bit nervous, and they started out with small talk, asking me how I felt and saying how much better I was looking and so on. I knew what was coming, but even so it came pretty abruptly.

"Mose Pathkiller seems to have gotten himself into quite a bit of trouble since you've been gone," said Daddy.

"Oh yeah?" I said, acting ignorant.

"It looks like he killed Ab Foster," said Daddy. He paused to let that soak in and, I think, to study my reaction. Then he went on.

"The day after you walked out of here, Ab had gone out to talk to Mose, and he didn't come back. He was found later out at Mose's place —dead. Mose had disappeared, so Harlan Tedford went out with some men to bring him in for questioning. He killed Tedford and one more deputy. Two of them got back, one shot pretty bad. It was Mose, sure enough. He called out to them and gave his name. Thurman Slimp led eight more of them out after him right after that, and Mose killed all nine of them. I don't know of anyone else who's ever done that. Nine lawmen killed by one man. Charlie, your friend has become the worst outlaw of our time—maybe all time. There's a thousand-dollar reward offered for Mose now, dead or alive, or for information leading to his capture."

"A thousand dollars, dead or alive?" I said, but it wasn't really a question.

"That's right, son," said Daddy, and he reached out to hand me a sheet of printed paper. I took it and saw that it was a handbill. It read like this:

REWARD
$1000
in gold coin
will be paid by the U.S. Government
for the apprehension
DEAD OR ALIVE
of
MOSES PATHKILLER

Wanted for the murders of deputies Abner Foster, Harlan Tedford, Thurman Slimp, and at least nine others, and other acts against the peace and dignity of the U.S.

DESCRIPTION
Moses Pathkiller is in his early twenties; 5 feet 8 inches high; weight about 165 to 170 lbs.; black hair, dark complexion, eyes black. He is a full-blooded Cherokee Indian, armed with a Winchester rifle, and is an excellent shot.

Send information to
Moss Berman,
Head of Deputies,
Fort Smith, Arkansas

Mama and Daddy were quiet for a bit, long enough to let me read the poster, and then Mama started talking again.

"Charlie," she said, "you can imagine how worried we were with you gone all this time and him doing all that killing out there. When you didn't come back and all this started to happen, why, we just didn't know what to think. We were worried that maybe you'd been killed."

"Charlie," said Daddy, looking real serious, "did Mose Pathkiller do this to you?"

Before I could stop myself, I was laughing. It was such an unexpected question that I just lost control of myself. I had been all prepared for accusations and questions concerning my whereabouts during all the time I had been missing. I was even afraid that they probably had it all properly put together, that they would be relatively certain that I had been with Mose the whole time. I sure wasn't prepared for what Daddy asked me.

"What's so funny, Charlie?" Daddy said.

"Daddy," I said, "how did I get here?"

"Why, I don't know, son. I thought that you had just somehow managed to get yourself on back home in spite of how bad off you were. I thought that you had knocked on the door and then passed out."

"Even if I had been in any condition to get myself home, which I wasn't, I couldn't have done it. I didn't have any idea where I was at."

"I don't understand," said Daddy. "We woke up in the middle of the night when we heard someone pounding on the door. Then I found you out on the porch, unconscious. This was there, too, along with your rifle and some other stuff from out at your cabin. We couldn't figure out what it was doing there. It has his name inside it."

He handed me a book, and I recognized it right away. I took it from him very carefully, like I was afraid it would break, and held it in both of my hands real close to my face. It was that damned Lord Byron, Mose's copy. In a couple of seconds, I carefully opened the front cover. There, in a careful and really a quite beautiful hand, he had written his name in the book—"Moses Pathkiller." I wondered if he had dropped it by mistake as he hauled me up on the porch, but that seemed unlikely. No, I decided. He must have left it on purpose for some reason. He was finished with it. But why? I lay the book down on my bedside table and took a deep breath.

"Mose brought me in, Daddy," I said. "If it hadn't been for Mose,

I'd still be out there in the hills somewhere, probably raving out of my head or maybe even dead."

"Mose Pathkiller brought you into town?"

"That's right, Daddy. If you'd been up just a little quicker, you might be a thousand dollars richer."

"But what happened to you? Where did Mose find you?"

"Daddy, you're not going to like this, but I've got to tell you the truth for once in my life. Mose didn't just happen to find me. I've been with him the whole time. This thing on my side is where one of those deputies shot right by me into some rocks, and a piece of rock hit me in the side. If I hadn't got hurt, I'd more than likely still be out there with him. I got sick and out of my head, and then I guess that Mose just figured that he had to get me back here where someone could take care of me. So he brought me home. He brought me in, in the wagon those deputies left out there. With a thousand dollars on his head and the whole territory swarming with lawmen, he drove right smack into town with me."

"Charlie," said Mama, "you don't mean that you were with him when he, well, when . . ."

"I've been with him the whole time," I said.

I thought that Mama was going to be hysterical for a minute there, but Daddy calmed her down some, or, at least, he quieted her down. He made her sit back down and told her to get ahold of herself, because this was no time to lose control. We might be in real trouble, and we needed to think things out. Then he looked at me, right in the face, real hard and long.

"Charlie, son," he said finally, "did you do any of the shooting?"

I wanted to tell him about the deputy whose head I split. I wanted to tell real bad, but I thought that for once in my life I had a reason for not saying what I wanted to say. I couldn't lie directly about it, though, not right then, right after I had said that I was going to tell him the truth this time.

"Mose never asked for my help in anything," I said. "All I went along for was just to keep him company."

"Oh, thank God," said Mama, "but what are we going to do?"

"Now I'm going to tell you," said Daddy. "I'm going to tell you, and I want you both to listen real good. Not one word of this is to go beyond these walls. Do you both understand that? Not one word.

There's been no word that I know of about anyone being out there with Mose. They're looking for him alone. It wouldn't matter any at all to the law that all you did was just to go along with Mose. If you were there when he killed any of those men, they could hang you, Charlie. Do you understand what I'm telling you?"

Well, Daddy had finally come through, but I couldn't help but feel that his reasons were all wrong. I didn't argue, though. The thought of the possibility of being hanged came very near to making me sick all over again. Daddy spread the word that I'd come wandering home late one night more dead than alive and out of my head. He said that none of us, including me, knew exactly what had happened to me, and that I was just lucky to have found my way home. The general opinion that formed around town was that Mose Pathkiller had probably shot me and left me for dead. I was soon thought to be one of the luckiest men in the Indian Territory to have survived the wrath of Mose Pathkiller, the meanest outlaw alive.

But I've been neglecting Velma.

Right after Daddy outlined our plans for me and Mama, and as soon as he felt that Mama was sufficiently calm, he went to see the Hotchkisses, to give them the good news. Needless to say, old Velma was overjoyed to learn that I was alive and well and back. She came straight back to the house with Daddy to see me. Daddy had given her his version of my recent misadventures, so I didn't have to tax myself too much with telling the tale to her. Anyway, she didn't seem very interested in what had happened to me, just in my present condition. And what concerned her the most about that was, would I be able to stand up through a wedding ceremony? I had been fortunate enough to make it back home just three days before the wedding date, which her mother had set that day I sent Velma home from the graveyard to make all the plans. The doctor was called in again. He said that I really should rest for about a week before I went to work or anything, but that he supposed that I would be able to go through the ceremony if it wasn't too long, and if I got right back to rest after it was done. He was only agreeing, he said, because he knew how much trouble it was to make plans for a wedding and then to have to rearrange them, but he said that it might be wise of us to postpone the honeymoon until the week was up. We all agreed to that.

I don't want to dwell on it, because it was a very bad experience for me and there was nothing at all interesting about it, even though Velma and her mama and mine all said that it was a lovely wedding, but I stood up through the goddamned ceremony on the scheduled date, and Velma and I were married. Right after it was all over, I was rushed back to my daddy's house and put back to bed, and Velma went back home to her folks. I thought that I should feel different somehow, and I was a little disappointed that I just felt the same way and that it didn't seem to mean anything to think that Velma was my wife, that she was Mrs. Charles Black, for God's sake. Anyway, I just stayed in bed for the rest of that week like the doctor said I should, and Velma came around once a day to visit with me and to see how I was feeling. Then one day toward the end of the period of my confinement, Daddy came in with a big surprise for me. For a wedding present, he and Mr. Hotchkiss had gone together and bought me and Velma a nice little house right in town, and our two mamas and Velma were right at that very moment over there working to get it in shape for us to move into just as soon as I was able to get up and out of bed. Then he told me that he had decided that I could probably use even another week off from work after all I had been through, and seeing as how I'd just been married and hadn't had a real honeymoon; but by the end of that week, he said, he was going to expect to see me at work bright and early on Monday morning. And to top it all off, he brought out some papers to show me. He had been to see Mr. Sanderson, the lawyer, and he had gotten papers that made me a full partner and said that when he died, the store would be all mine, and he said that he had a man down at the store that very day changing the sign out front to read "Black & Black."

At the end of that week, I moved into my new house with Velma, and at the end of the next one, I went to work in my store.

CHAPTER TWENTY-THREE

Listen.
Now I have come to step over your soul.

Your spittle I have put at rest under the earth.
Your soul I have put at rest under the earth.
I have come to cover you over with the black rock.
I have come to cover you over with the black cloth.
I have come to cover you over with black slabs,
never to reappear.
Toward the black coffin of the upland
in the Darkening Land
your paths shall stretch out.
So shall it be for you.
The clay of the upland has come to cover you.
Instantly the black clay
has lodged there where it is
at the black houses
in the Darkening Land.
With the black coffin
and the black slabs
I have come to cover you.
Now your soul has faded away.
It has become blue.
When darkness comes
your spirit shall become less and dwindle away,
never to reappear.
Listen.

During the first week I was up and about, I was real surprised one day to see Sarah walking along the side of Main Street with a bundle of supplies in her arms. It wouldn't have been surprising except for the fact that Sarah lives so far away, and even if she had needed to go somewhere for supplies, there were little towns and country stores that were much closer to her place than Tahlequah was. I had never seen her in town before in my whole life. I was curious to find out if she had any news concerning Mose. So I watched where she went, and when she headed out of town again I followed her, far enough back so that nobody in town would notice. I caught up with her a little ways out of town.

"Hey, Sarah," I called out to her, "wait up a bit, will you?"

She stopped in her tracks and whirled around, looking a little frightened.

"Charlie?" she said. "Charlie Blackbird, that you?"

"Yes, Sarah. I want to talk to you for a minute."

I had walked up even with her by then. She looked off down the road the direction we both had come from, and I did, too. There was no one in sight. She motioned for me to follow her off the road into some thick trees where we wouldn't be seen. When we got to where we felt hidden in the trees, we sat down on the ground.

"Have you seen Mose, Sarah?" I asked her.

She just looked at me, I thought, a little suspiciously.

"Sarah," I said, "for God's sake. It's me. I've been with him out there. I even killed one of them deputies."

"I'm sorry, Charlie," she finally said. "I know you're okay. It's just that I been so worried for Mose, you know? After he carried you back home when you was hurt, he come back for me. I been with him since then."

"Well, what the hell were you doing in town then?"

"Trying to find out about them laws in there, you know? I found out a lot, too, Charlie."

"Listen, Sarah," I said, "you've got to tell Mose to get the hell away from here. There's a thousand-dollar reward offered for him, dead or alive, and there's more and more laws gathering around here all the time. Not only that, but with that reward poster up all over the place, there's no telling who all will go out there after him now. He ain't safe around here. Tell him to go somewhere, will you? Someplace far off. And you go with him and take care of him."

She waited a minute before she answered me, and she was looking down at the ground. I felt like she would have liked to have given me a different answer.

"I got to do like Mose says, Charlie. Mose told me to find out about the laws in Tahlequah. I found out and I'll tell him. When he knows, he'll kill them all. Just like that no-good Slimp."

"What do you know about Slimp, Sarah? Mose and me didn't even know who that was out there. I just found out after he brought me back to town."

"That no-good Slimp came to my house," she said, and her eyes narrowed. "He came with eight more laws and said they would sleep in my house. I said no. He pushed me in the house and come in anyway. He slept on my bed. All the others on the floor. I didn't sleep all night. Just sat up and watched. Come morning they eat all my eggs, all my bacon, bread, coffee. Even made me cook."

She stopped here to spit and then continued.

"What they don't eat, Slimp stole. Put it in bags and took it out to the wagon. I grabbed his arm one time and called him no-good thief. He hit me in the face. Before he left, he asked me do I know Mose. I said yes. He asked me do I know where Mose is at. I said no, but I said I wish him good luck to find Mose. I said I hope he finds Mose, because when he finds Mose, Mose will kill him. Right between the eyes, I told him. Slimp just laughed, you know? But when Mose came back for me, he told me about nine laws. I know."

"Sarah, can I see him?"

"No, Charlie. It ain't safe, you know?"

"But, Sarah . . ."

"Charlie, it can't even do you no good. Mose, he won't talk English no more, you know? No more."

I remembered the book then, and it all seemed to make a little more sense, like maybe he had finally rejected everything white.

"Okay, Sarah," I said, and I begged her once again to tell Mose what I had said, to get him out of the territory as far as possible, where he might be safe from the lawmen gathering around the area all looking for him. She promised to tell him, but she said that she didn't expect that he would go anywhere. I knew that she was right. Where would he go? Especially since he would no longer speak anything but Cherokee. I had a strange feeling come over me, like it was dark and heavy and there was nothing anybody could do about it. Then Sarah left to go on her way back to Mose, and I went on back into town.

During the previous week, while I had still been in bed, one of the most impressive fighting forces that folks in our part of the country had ever seen or even heard of was gathering in Tahlequah, using the office that had been Foster's as headquarters. These were the lawmen that Sarah had been spying on for Mose, that she and I had talked about. Before they were through building up their strength for the action against Mose, they had become seventeen strong, and they were mostly well-known and respected lawmen. They were headed up by U.S. Marshal Moss Berman, and Bill Green, A. B. Washburn, Ike Maggitt and Pepper Winston were among the deputies in the group. It created quite a stir, having the whole lot of them around for all that time in our town. They went out from time to time and asked questions of the full-bloods in the hills, including old Malachi, trying to get a line on Mose, but not until they had built themselves up to full strength did they actually move out to get on his trail. That was after Velma and I had moved into our house, during our first week there. They had been gone for one whole week when they finally rode back into town. Three of them were in the back of the wagon they had taken along with them—dead. Three others were shot up some but were able to ride back in by themselves. The remaining eleven just looked a little worse for the wear, but weren't hurt. It was all I could do to keep myself from rushing out to meet them to find out what I could about Mose.

I was working in the store when they rode back into town, so I only had to wait a little while before Marshal Berman came in to replenish their ammunition supply. Daddy met him at the door.

"Afternoon, Marshal," said Daddy. "What can I do for you?"

Berman handed him a list.

"Just fill this order for me, if you please, Mr. Black."

"Right away," said Daddy, and he set about getting what was needed off the shelves while he continued the conversation.

"Looks like you ran into a little trouble out there," he said.

"Lost three good men," said the marshal. "Three more hurt. They'll be all right, but they ain't going to be much use to me for a while."

"I take it you found him, though."

"We found the son of a bitch all right. But he saw us coming, and he was waiting for us. Hid out in a clump of trees up on the side of a hill. We didn't know what the hell had hit us until six was done shot. The rest of us opened fire on him right away, and I think I got him."

"You got him?" I asked.

"Yeah. That's when he took off. I think I got him in the neck, but not good enough. That's what makes me so goddamned mad. It just wasn't good enough."

"You mean he got away then?"

"Yeah, he got away, God damn him to hell. He took off in them damned woods until we couldn't follow him on horseback, and then we had three bodies and three wounded to take care of. Anyways, we was about out of supplies, and it seemed like the best thing to do was to come on back in here and kind of reorganize."

Daddy put all the stuff up on the counter.

"Well, you'll be going back out, won't you?" he asked.

"I figure in about another week. I figure this time we'll take us enough supplies to stay out yonder for a whole goddamn month if need be, and we'll take enough men along so if someone gets himself hurt, we won't have to call off the whole damn thing."

He signed the bill and gathered up the stuff and left. By the end of the week, he not only had replacements for the three dead and the three wounded, but he also had an additional six deputies, bringing the total up to twenty-three. They had been in town for only a couple of days before Berman came back over to the store. This time he brought a wagon and had us load it up with all the supplies he thought they would need for a month. It looked to me like Mose would have his work cut out for him either to fight or to hide from this bunch. I hoped that, after his recent scrape with this newest gang of lawmen, he had decided to take my advice and get the hell out of the territory, but down deep, I knew better. Berman was at the counter just about to sign for all the supplies when the door opened, and he just kind of glanced up the way anyone will do to see who's just walked into a room.

"Hold this just a bit, will you, Mr. Black?" he said to Daddy. "I just remembered a couple of things I maybe forgot."

"What are they?" said Daddy. "I'll help you find them, and we'll get them loaded up for you."

"Oh, naw," said Berman. "Just let me look around a bit first."

What he was doing was he was stalling around, because he had seen who had just come into the store. It was old Malachi. He hadn't been into town for years, and at first I didn't know quite how to react, but then I decided to move real fast to see what he wanted rather than let Daddy get to him first.

" *'Siyo*, Malachi," I said. "It's good to see you."

"I come in to buy some of them bullets, .30-.30," he said.

He pulled a couple of bills from his pocket.

"All right, Malachi. Right over here."

I walked around to the other side of the counter, where we kept the shells.

"You haven't been into town for a long time," I said.

"My two boys is gone," he said. "I get really hungry sometimes. Need some .30-.30 bullets to hunt."

"Well," I said, "here you are. And I wish you good hunting."

He looked me straight in the face, like he and I both knew something that the others didn't, and then he took the shells in his left hand, turned and walked out of the store. It struck me then that those shells were for Mose, and that he was still out there at the cabin. Just out there at the cabin. At home. He hadn't paid a damn bit of attention to what I had said, assuming that Sarah had even bothered to relay the message. If he had left the area at all, it had been only temporarily, just to lead those lawmen around some. Twenty-three of the most deadly men in the territory right here within easy walking distance of him. God damn him, I thought, the damn fool. Then I heard Berman.

"That there was old Malachi Pathkiller, wasn't it, Mr. Black?"

"Yeah," said Daddy. "Real strange, too. I haven't seen him in town for years."

"It's not really so strange," I said. "He used to have two sons living with him to come in to fetch stuff. Now they're both gone, he's got no choice but to come in himself."

"Well now," said Berman, "where'd that old bastard get any cash money, I wonder?"

I was about to try to invent some plausible answer for his question, but he just kept talking.

"And how's he planning to do any hunting with a rifle with only one good arm and that his left one, huh?"

"He's left-handed," I said, "and a damn good shot, too."

Berman put his name on the bill and left the store in a big hurry. I don't think that my answers to his questions about Malachi impressed him a bit. I ran to the window and saw him on his way into the office the deputies were using as their headquarters. In a few minutes, all twenty-three of them were on their horses and on the way out of town in the direction of old Malachi's cabin.

CHAPTER TWENTY-FOUR

For the next hour and a half, I wasn't worth a damn in the store. I kept knocking things over, and when I got a customer, I added his bill up wrong and overcharged him. The only thing that kept him from thinking that I was trying to cheat him was the fact that I looked so nervous. Daddy finally just told me to stay out of the way until I could control myself. Things weren't so busy right then, anyway.

Then Bill Green came into the store. He was kind of hurrying, but not really too much. Daddy met him about halfway between the counter and the door.

"What can I do for you, Mr. Green?" he said.

"Dynamite, Mr. Black. You got any?"

"Why, yes. I've got it. Aren't you supposed to be . . ."

"I'm on duty right now, Mr. Black. Marshal Berman sent me in here to get some dynamite off of you. Oh, here. He give me this here note."

Daddy took the piece of paper away from Green and read it.

"All right," he said. "This seems to be in order. How much do you want?"

"Just give me half a dozen sticks and mark it up for us."

Daddy went to the back of the store to get the stuff, and I walked out to the edge of the counter so I could talk to Green.

"Mr. Green," I said, "what's happening out there?"

"We got him this time, by God," said Green. "We followed the old man back out to his house, and when we got kind of close, Pathkiller must have heard us coming, because we seen him break out of the house and run like hell through the woods. But we was right on his ass this time, and we cornered him in another old cabin just a short piece from there."

I figured that must be Mose's old cabin.

"And he's still in there?" I asked.

"He's still in there, and he ain't going to go nowhere either. We got him completely surrounded. There ain't no way out of there."

"Well, what's the dynamite for?"

"Hell, he won't come out of that damn cabin, and we can't shoot him out of it. We just been sitting out there on our ass wasting god-damn ammunition, and he's done picked off two men."

Daddy came back with the dynamite, and he started to write out the bill for Green to sign.

"This will bring him out, by God," said Green.

Daddy turned the bill around on the counter and handed Green the pencil. Green struggled real hard to get his name on it.

"Mr. Green," I said, "can I ride out there with you?"

"Hell, boy, I don't see no reason why not. I think half the goddamn town's out there already just to watch the fireworks."

Green clutched his bundle of dynamite sticks and went out the door.

"Charlie," said Daddy, "do you know what you're doing?"

"I think so, Daddy. I'm really not doing anything. I just think that I ought to be there, you know?"

"All right, son," he said. I don't think that it was all right with him, but he must have known that I was going no matter what he thought about it or what he said.

I hurried down the street to rent myself a horse, and I caught up with Bill Green before he was halfway back to the cabin. When we got out there, there were people all around the place. There must have been more casual spectators than there were lawmen, just standing around watching. We found out that since Green had left on his er-rand, Mose had gotten two more of them. One of them was just one of the spectators, and I couldn't help but feel that it served the son of a bitch right. After all, what had he gone out there for but to watch somebody else get killed? At the time I got there with Green, Mose wasn't firing at all, and I wondered if he had gotten the ammunition from old Malachi before he had to run from the old man's cabin. The deputies were firing occasionally into the windows, but Mose was staying out of sight. When we rode up just to the rear of the line, Green yelled out real loud.

"Hey, Marshal, I got it. I got the stuff."

Mose popped up in the window just then and sent a slug into the side of Green's face. Then he disappeared again real fast, and a barrage of shots from the laws followed. Most of them thunked harmlessly into the logs of the cabin wall. It didn't make any sense for everyone to be shooting like that, because Mose was out of sight again, but they were. I heard Berman's voice over all the noise finally shouting.

"Hold your fire. Hold your fire, God damn it."

Then the shooting stopped again. I was keeping low behind some bushes back where most of the horses were and where Green had fallen with the dynamite sticks, and Berman and Pepper Winston came running over to where I was at. They hardly even noticed me. Berman picked up the dynamite sticks.

"Pepper," he said, "you think you can work your way up to the cabin and plant these goddamn things where they'll do some good?"

"I'll damn well try it, Moss."

"Well, look," said Berman, "see if you can't get them right on either side of that damn window right down close to the ground. That ought to take that whole goddamn wall down, and then we can open up on him from out here."

"Okay, Moss."

Winston took a cigar out of his pocket and lit it. He took a few puffs to get it going good, then he tied the sticks of dynamite into two bundles of three each and turned toward the cabin. He jumped up and took off running as fast as he could go, all crouched down, until he got close enough to the cabin to just sort of dive for the wall. He smashed into the wall just at ground level, and he very quickly jammed one of the bundles under the lowest log and lit the fuse with his cigar. Then he quickly moved to the other side of the window and did the same thing there. He straightened up enough to start running back for cover, and Mose appeared in the window again and sent one shot into Winston's ass, real low, and where it came out in front, well, I never knew if Pepper Winston was a family man or not, but if he wasn't already, he never will be. Anyway, just as before, there was a terrific barrage of shots into the empty window where Mose had just been, and just as Winston went crashing to the ground on his face right at the feet of Moss Berman and screaming at the top of his lungs, there was a horrible blast that showered us all with dirt and sticks and was followed real fast by a second blast. I covered my head to keep from getting my eyes put out by all the flying trash, and when I raised it up again, the air was still so thick with smoke and dirt that I could hardly even see the cabin. Then, about where the wall should have been, appeared a shadowy figure, staggering just a little through the haze. It had to be Mose. He was holding his rifle, but not like he was getting ready to use it. It was across his chest like he was just carrying it easy and holding it ready. Everyone else must have seen him just about the same time I did, because all of a sudden it sounded like a war just started. But now I think about it, it was really the end of a war—of Mose's private war. I thought they were never going to stop shooting and let him fall, but they finally did, and then they all got out from behind their cover to run up and get a good look at what they had killed.

"Well, that does it," I heard Moss Berman say.

"Yeah, the son of a bitch."

"Hey, Moss," said someone whose voice I didn't know, "his goddamn rifle's empty. How about that?"

I turned and walked slowly back to my rented horse, climbed wearily into the saddle and started back to town.

CHAPTER TWENTY-FIVE

When the army of deputies rode back into town, they brought Mose with them. They took him inside their headquarters, and then they tied him to a long slab. They pulled his arms up across his chest and tied the wrists together, and then they put his rifle in his arms. They took the slab with Mose on it to the front window of the office building and propped it up there so that everyone could walk by and see the notorious outlaw, Mose Pathkiller, looking (as much as possible) like he had in real life when he had been such a terror to territorial lawmen. George Sweet took his camera over there and set it up in the street so he could get a picture of Mose standing there in the window. They left him there overnight and then took him to Fort Smith so they could receive their official commendations. I understand that they stopped in one or two towns along the way, to stand Mose up for the local citizens to get a look at. When they were all done with him, they shipped him back to us, that is, to Tahlequah, and old Malachi came into town for the second time in all those years—this time to take his last son home one more time.

A couple of years passed. Velma and I had a small son. I never did get along well with the kid. He was so pale and white that he made me sick, and when he tried to talk, he whined like his mother did. But everyone said that he was a very sweet kid and that he looked just like his daddy. Velma was soon fat and pregnant again, and I was doing very well for us with the store. Most people forgot that I had ever known Mose Pathkiller. I never went back to my cabin, but I had a nice home in town, and I managed to set aside quite a bit in savings. I had a Sunday school class at the Baptist church in town and was becoming one of the leading citizens of the community, and I think that I might have learned to live with it and even to fool myself into thinking I was happy if I could only have got that picture of Mose roped to that goddamned slab out of my mind.

CHAPTER TWENTY-SIX

I had just about resigned myself to my fate with Velma and our white kid when something happened to me that changed everything. I mean, something happened inside of me, and I don't know really how to explain it. I do know just about when it happened, though, and some of the things that were going on about that time. For one thing, old Velma really changed. Like one night when I really wanted to make love to her and she just lay there like she was dead. I kept feeling around on her, trying to make her want it too for what seemed like forever, and I didn't get any response at all until she finally opened her yap.

"Charlie Black," she said, "how do you expect me to get any sleep with you pawing at me?"

"The name is Blackbird," I said. I don't know what I meant by that or why I said it at that time, but I just turned over in the bed and made like I was going on to sleep, but I didn't go on to sleep, and tears came into my eyes. I remember thinking that a man shouldn't have to live like that. She'd been that way before, but somehow it was what she said and the way she'd said it that made it hurt so bad that particular time. I thought that I ought to rape her, but I knew that I wouldn't really do it. I didn't sleep much at all that night. I thought about living with Velma. I thought about our kid that I really didn't like. But most of all, I thought about how all my life I'd been thinking about what I'd like to say or like to do or even believed that I ought to do, and that I'd never done it. I'd always done something else. I'd always done what Daddy or Mama or Velma or somebody besides me thought that I ought to be doing.

The next morning, I didn't fuss or anything, but I didn't say any more to her than I had to, and I got off to work just as quick as I could.

I thought that maybe work would take my mind off Velma, but as it turned out, something else took my mind off work and Velma for most of the day. Daddy came in pretty early that morning.

"Charlie," he said, as he came rushing through the front door.

"Morning, Daddy," I said.

"Charlie," Daddy went on, "have you heard the news?"

"I guess not. What news is that?"

"The Dawes Commission people are in town, and they're signing up all Cherokees for allotments."

"Oh," I said.

"Is that all you can say? You know what that means, Charlie? Land. Free land. And land is money. There'll be land for me and land for your mama and land for you. Land for Velma, too. All we got to do is go down and sign up. Why, you can even get it for your boy. I'm going on down and sign up, and when I get done, I'll come right on back here and let you go."

He had already started back for the door, but I stopped him.

"Daddy," I said, "hold up a minute."

He turned back around to face me with a puzzled look on his face. I went on.

"How come you all of a sudden so all-fired hot about being a Indian? All my life, I listened to you talk about them full-bloods. Lazy Indians. Worthless. Telling me to stay away from the best friends I ever had. Always taking the white man's side against the Indians. You remember all that? Then how come all of a sudden you so anxious to write yourself down a Cherokee?"

He stood there, his hand on the door handle, looking at me. He didn't answer me right away. He just looked at me with an expression I'd never seen on his face before. He looked as if he really hated me. He looked like he could have killed me.

"Well," I said, "tell me."

"Charlie," he said, kind of through his teeth, "I'm not going back on a thing I ever said. But we've got Cherokee blood, and we are entitled to that land. What's more, from what I hear, the full-bloods don't want it, anyway. The commissioners are having to track them down out in the hills and beg them or threaten them to get them to sign up."

"It ain't that they don't want it," I said. "They already own it. They own it altogether. They don't want it in allotments, and they don't want to lose all that the government's going to declare excess and sell to whites."

"Well, Charlie, I don't want to argue with you about it. The fact is it's happening, whether you like it or not, whether it's right or wrong. It's happening, and you can either take advantage of it or get left behind. And if you're too bullheaded to take advantage of it, then there may not be any hope for you after all."

He went out and slammed the door behind himself so hard that I thought the glass would break, but it didn't. I stood there and I felt myself shaking.

"Son of a bitch," I said.

I knew that many of the full-bloods, the traditional people, people like old Shalleloski, who had very likely saved my life that time I was out with Mose and I got sick, and even people like old Malachi, would not sign the roll unless they were forced to, because they knew that its purpose was the allotment of lands to individuals, the breakup of tribal lands and the eventual dissolution of the Cherokee Nation. My old man knew all that too, but he thought that it was primitive. He thought that the traditionals' not believing in private ownership of land was a kind of savage Bolshevism. I'd heard him say that lots of times.

Anyway, I was so mad that I didn't want to be there when Daddy got back. I felt like all of a sudden, after all those years, I just couldn't stand to listen to him anymore. I had to get out. I couldn't go home either. I couldn't stand to face Velma after the way she'd done me the night before. I don't know. I've thought about this a lot over the years, trying to figure myself out. I'd put up with Daddy and Velma for so long that I don't know what it was about that day that I was finally fed up. But I was. I didn't know what to do, and I was shaking worse than ever, I was so mad. Then I got a crazy urge. I walked to the back of the store and got a tall ladder and took it out front on the sidewalk and set it up just beneath the big "Black & Black" sign that Daddy'd been so proud of, and I went back inside and got a bucket of paint and a brush and I painted "bird" after the second "Black" so that the sign read "Black & Blackbird." Then I climbed back down and started to put the ladder up, but I was so mad I fumbled around and spilled the bucket of paint on the sidewalk. I just threw the bucket down, and then for the first time I noticed that old man Lawson and a few others from the street were standing out in front of their places looking at me.

"It's Blackbird," I shouted at them.

Then I walked off down the street in a hurry. I had no place in mind, but soon I found myself in Sam Billings' place, and I had a drink, but some other people from town came in, and I got more nervous. I didn't want to have to talk to them, and just anyone might come in Sam's place, so I left. Just outside of town, there was another place, like Sam's, but trashier. It was owned by a white man named Jud. I never heard his other name. For all I know he never had one. When I got there, I saw three men passed out in the yard and two more sitting on the porch looking as if they would soon join the other three. I walked right by them and opened the door. There was five or six guys in there, all white men, sitting on chairs and leaning on tables. Jud was off in a corner, sitting on a whiskey keg. His elbows were on his knees, and he was holding a length of log chain and just watching. When I walked in, everybody looked at me.

"Looks as if you're open for business all right," I said to Jud.

"Well," he said, "this sure ain't no social gathering."

"Give me some whiskey then," I said, and I tossed some cash on the counter.

Jud got up and walked around behind the counter to fetch me a jug.

"You don't get out here much," he said. "I figured you was too snitty for us out here."

I took a drink, and it burned my guts.

"Shit," I said.

"You rich breeds don't get around us poor white trash much. You got your pockets full of money tonight?"

"I paid you for your goddamned rotgut whiskey," I said. "That's all you need to know."

I picked up my jug and walked over to the keg Jud had been using for a chair and sat down on it. Everyone in the room was looking at me. I took another drink. It didn't taste any better than the first.

"You a breed?"

The voice came from a big redhead across the room from me. I took another drink. There was a slight improvement in taste with the third swallow.

"Hey," said the redhead, raising his voice, "you a breed?"

"I'm a Cherokee Indian," I said.

"One of them rich ones," said Jud. "He's a storekeeper in Tahle-quah."

"A rich Indian, huh?" said the redhead. "Going to get richer, too, I reckon. Hey, how much land you get for signing up on that thing? You get a bunch of land?"

"I didn't get none of it," I said. "Nothing. And I don't want to talk about it."

"None of it? How come you didn't get none of it, if you're a god-damned Indian? How come?"

"Because I won't sign their goddamned roll," I said.

"Is that all you got to do?" said the redhead. "Sign the roll? I'll sign the son of a bitch. Where do I got to go? I'm part Cherokee. Where do I go?"

"You're no Cherokee," I said. "You're a damned liar, and I doubt if you can write your own name. Now leave me alone."

The redhead looked as if he wanted to squash my head, but he didn't say anything. Instead, he got up and walked over to Jud. They started talking real low. I couldn't hear them, but I felt like they were talking about me. I began to feel just a bit edgy. I took another drink. The redhead walked back to his chair, but all the way he had his eyes on me. I took another drink. It tasted good. It got quiet all of a sudden in Jud's place, and it stayed that way for a while, I don't know how long, but I kept drinking, and they kept watching me, and I began to feel some-what woozy. I had just enough sense about me to remember thinking to myself what a goddamn fool I was for being there, for getting myself drunk in there, and for talking to those rednecks the way I did. And I know to this day, that if they had left me alone, I would have staggered on home and fell in bed and got up the next day and gone on about my life the way I always done before. But that ain't what happened.

I kind of leaned forward, and when I did, I like to have turned over on the floor, because the keg I was sitting on, I found out, was empty. I caught my balance, though, and sat back up straight again, just in time to see the redhead walking across the room again. This time, though, he got about halfway across and angled over toward me. I can't say exactly what my thoughts were, because they came kind of jumbled and fast, but I thought that he might be coming for me, to kill me, or at least to whip me, and to get my money. I felt of the keg around the edge, and I found the hole where the spigot had been, and I stuck my thumb in it. Then I leaned forward again, just enough to get my butt off the keg a little bit. I tried to make it look like I still had my weight on it and like I wasn't paying no mind to the redhead. Then, when he was just about three steps away, I come up to my feet, and I swung that keg for all I was worth. I caught the redhead just across the side of his face, and it made an awful sound and slung blood clean over on Jud behind the counter. The redhead never made a sound. He just dropped. Jud yelled, though, and he dropped out of sight behind the counter. The two men nearest me in the room came up out of their chairs. I don't know if they were coming for me or just fixing to get out of the way, but I wasn't taking no chances. I brought that keg around again, and I got them both. Then I saw Jud come up again from behind the counter, and he had a shotgun. I threw the keg at him and kicked over a table and ducked behind it just in time. Jud recovered his composure and blasted both barrels at me, and splinters flew all over the room. One of the guys I'd laid low was laying on the floor just by me, and I saw a hogleg sticking out of his waistband. I jerked it out and stood up, holding it at arm's length in front of me with both hands, and I blasted Jud square in the chest. The force of it knocked him back into the wall, and he slid down to the floor, disappearing once more behind his counter.

Then I turned to face the rest of the room. Someone had just run out the door, I don't know how many, but there were two left standing across the room from me. I can't say what they were doing, but I was moving too fast to wonder at the time. I shot them both.

I hadn't drank all that much booze, but I guess that what I had drank had got to my head. Or maybe what really had got to my head was what I had just done. I stood there with that gun in my hand just looking around the room, looking at the bodies and the blood. And I felt woozy, but I felt good, too. I felt better than I had felt since I'd been out with Mose that time we were on the scout, and I had killed that damned lawman. I felt like, well, I felt like—Mose. Damn me, but I felt good.

I stuck that pistol in my waistband, and I picked up my jug, and I went out onto the porch. The only signs of life were from the three drunks who were passed out. I sat down heavy on the porch and commenced to get my money's worth out of that jug.

When I came to, the sun was high and I was sweating. My head was throbbing like hell. There was one drunk still laying there in his own puke and passed out, but the other two were gone. Then I recalled that I had let two others run out of the room when the shooting had started. Someone is bound to call the laws, I thought.

And then I saw that what I had never been able to sit down and talk myself into doing, I had done without thinking about it. The laws were bound to get after me for this. There was not only the two drunks but them that had run out the night before during the shooting. One of the four must have known me or at least have been able to give a good enough description. I had to go on the scout. This time it would be me. This time would have to be for good. There would be no more going back to Daddy this time. And there wouldn't be any more putting up with Daddy, nor with Velma, nor with that damned kid of Velma's— Velma's, not mine. There wouldn't be any more storekeeping. No more Sunday school. And there wouldn't be any more putting up with shit from anybody. Just like I hadn't put up with nothing from those drunk whites. And best of all, there wouldn't be no more living like a white man.

CHAPTER TWENTY-SEVEN

When my head started to clear a little, I realized that I was just sitting there, waiting for the laws to come for me. I had to get out. I tucked the pistol I had used inside into my trousers and started walking. I didn't really have any place in mind to go to. I couldn't go out in the woods the way Mose had done, because I didn't know my way around out there the way he did. I stayed pretty close to the road and headed south. One time I got tired and my head was hurting, so I crawled off into the bushes and slept for a little. Then I walked again until it was starting to get dark. I was hungry, too, and I decided that I needed a horse. Then I realized that old man Lawson's place was just up the road from me, maybe a quarter of a mile. I owed him something for Mose, so I decided to get me a horse from him. Maybe some guns, too. I walked on up close to Lawson's house and sat down to wait for it to get good and late.

When the lights were all out, I sneaked on down there and went out back to the corral. I found me a good saddle and some tack in the tack house, and then I caught me a good-looking horse out of the corral and saddled him up. I remembered that old Lawson hated dogs, and that gave me a little laugh. I led the horse across the road and thought about going on down to the house and stealing whatever guns the old son of a bitch might have in the house, but something kept me from it, and I just mounted up and headed on down the road. I had a horse and a gun but no bullets. I'd emptied the gun back at Jud's place.

I didn't really pick Muskogee. I was just headed southwest along that road, and that's where it led me. I had to go somewhere. When I finally rode into Muskogee on a stolen horse with a stolen gun in my pants, my storekeeper's clothes all dirty and wrinkled, I was tired and hungry, and I stank. I did have a little cash on me, so I found a place to get a bath, and I bought me some new clothes. I bought a box of shells for the revolver, and then I went to the nearest restaurant to get something to eat. I ordered eggs and bacon and biscuits. I was drinking my coffee and waiting for my meal when a big white man walked in. He looked mad as hell, and he was looking around for something or for someone. Then I noticed that he didn't have shoes on. When he spotted a man sitting at a table behind me, he straightened himself up and walked toward that man. I looked around to see who he was after, just out of curiosity. The man at the table was almost as big as the barefooted white man. He looked like a black man to me, but I couldn't be sure. His skin wasn't really dark. He might have been mixed. And he had the biggest breakfast I ever did see for one man on the table in front of him.

"Hey, you," the white man said, just about the time he walked past me.

The other one didn't look up from his breakfast.

"I'm talking to you, you yellow nigger," said the white man.

The man stopped eating his breakfast and looked up from the table slowly. The waiter looked out from the kitchen door. I stayed half-turned in my chair so I could watch.

"Hey," called the waiter, "we don't want no trouble in here."

"That there son of a bitch is wearing my boots," said the big white man.

The other guy looked down at his feet and kind of grinned, and he did have on a shiny pair of black boots that didn't exactly seem to fit with the rest of his shabby outfit.

"You know what he's talking about?" asked the waiter.

"Hell," said the one with the boots, "I ain't never seen this man before."

The big barefooted guy was carrying a rolled-up newspaper under his arm, and he stomped on over to the other fellow's table and threw that paper down on it.

"Them's my damn boots you got on, boy," he said, "and if you pull them off and give them back to me right now, I might not even whip your black ass for stealing them."

The man with the boots suddenly jumped up to his feet, grabbed the newspaper the other had tossed down on the table, and slapped the barefoot man three times hard across the face with it.

"I'm a Cherokee Indian, you son of a bitch," he said, "and you better apologize to me while you still can."

The big man was caught off-guard, but he came out of it quick enough. He kicked over the table and drew out a long-bladed knife from somewhere, but as he started to move with it toward the other guy, I hauled out my stolen .44 and pulled the hammer back.

"Hold it, mister," I said.

The big man stopped still.

"Now, drop that knife back behind you."

He did. Then I got up and kicked the knife across the room.

"You still want him to apologize?" I asked.

"He had his chance. It's too late now."

The black Cherokee swung a fist into the big man's guts, but it didn't do as much damage as he had figured it would. The big man grabbed him by the arm and swung him around into the wall, then drove two fists, one after the other, into his ribs. The black Cherokee drew his arms in close to his chest to protect his body from those hard punches and his fists up in front of his face to protect it. He took several of those blows that way. Then he saw his chance, and he raised his knee up and then stomped down as hard as he could onto that white man's bare foot, and I swear that I heard some bones crack. The big man screamed and picked his foot up off the floor, grabbing for it with his hands, and when he did that, he caught a terrific blow on his ear. He staggered back a few steps, and the black Cherokee lifted the nearest chair and bashed him over the head with it. The big man fell like a flour sack.

"Help me throw this bastard out in the street," the Cherokee said.

I got up and helped him drag the man to the door and pitch him out. Then, since his table had been overturned, I invited him to sit with me.

"I'm Solomon Web," he said. "What's your name?"

"Charlie Blackbird," I said, and I liked the sound of the old name.

"Blackbird? You Indian?"

"Yeah," I said. "Cherokee."

"I wondered why you helped me out just then."

"I don't think you really needed much help," I said.

I kind of liked the big man, even if he was black. I know that a lot of Indians, just like whites, don't have no use for blacks, but the way I look at it, I'm Indian, and the blacks never did anything for the Indians to be down on them for. It's always the whites that have been doing to the Indians. So it doesn't make sense for an Indian to think less of a black than of a white. I've known Indians that would whip a black man for saying that he was Indian or part Indian, but what the hell? There's Indian and white mixed, and there's Indian and black mixed. And since I think that the whites are worse than the blacks, why, that means that I'm worse than Solomon, because I'm part white and he's part black.

Anyhow, I did like him, and I sure did like the way he had whipped that big white man, but there was something I was real curious about.

"Say," I said, "about them boots . . ."

Solomon Web leaned back until his chair was just on its two back legs, and he laughed so hard I thought he was going to tumble over.

"I stole them off that white man while he was sleeping in the boardinghouse down the street here last night."

I laughed with him. When we had both finally stopped laughing, I leaned over to get a good look at the boots.

"It's a fine-looking pair of boots," I said.

Well, pretty soon we decided between the two of us that maybe we had ought to get out of town, seeing as how Solomon had, in fact, stole the man's boots, and then had beat him up somewhat, and that I had in a way helped him by pulling out my old stolen .44. There was also a matter of a broken table and chair and a few dishes. So we got on out of there and got our horses and rode out of town a ways, and we went down by the Arkansas River to set and talk and figure out what to do next. As it turned out, we were both footloose and fancy-free and both sick of putting up with the white people in towns. I kind of let old Sol know that I had done something outside of the law, but I didn't give any details, and he sort of responded in kind. I guess we were kind of feeling each other out, each one wanting to know how the other would feel about joining forces to go out and commit some outrages on the general public, or some such thing, and as it turned out, that's just what we decided to do. But we agreed that we wouldn't be outlaws, that we wouldn't hurt or rob or do any kind of wrong to Indians of whatever tribe. And that was the start of what was to become my second career.

CHAPTER TWENTY-EIGHT

We spent a couple of days just laying out along the Arkansas River, and we did a little fishing and a lot of talking. Old Sol told me about how he had been a harness maker with a little shop right there in Muskogee, and how, even though he was charged exorbitant rent for his little shop, mainly because he was black, he had still managed to save him up a little money to fix up his house with. It wasn't hardly even a house, the way he told it, but he had knocked the boards together solid and had put a couple of coats of paint on it. And then his troubles really began. Sol said that the good white folks of Muskogee didn't think that no nigger ought to have a nice house, and the first thing that happened was that his rent was doubled. Then folks stopped giving him their business. Pretty soon, he was busted.

Well, he said, that taught him his lesson. He wasn't going to be allowed to work hard at an honest trade and try to get ahead. So why work hard? Why be honest? Well, I couldn't argue with that. Besides, it sounded too much to me like what had happened to Mose with old man Lawson, and I told Sol that story. He just kind of nodded his head.

"Um hum," he said, "that's the way it is."

After a while Sol told me that he knew a few more fellows in the area that he said thought the same way we did, because they had been done dirty by white folks, too. If I was to agree, he said, they'd 'most for sure join up with us to pull some jobs.

"That is," he said, "if you're dead-set on taking up this here criminal life."

"Sol," I said, "I ain't hardly got no choice no more. In spite of my appearance and what some folks think, I ain't no white man, and there ain't hardly nothing for a man no more, if he ain't white. And there's more than that."

I sat quiet for a spell, and Sol didn't push me for details, but then I was beginning to feel close to him in a way that I hadn't felt close to anyone since Mose and Henry. Oh, it wasn't the same, but it was kind of like that. And he had talked straight to me, so I thought that it wouldn't do any harm, and then I told him everything. Not just how I came to be in Muskogee, but all about me and Mose, and how that I had been with Mose and had even shot one of the deputies that Mose had been credited with killing, and Mose had been made notorious with tall tales and such, so Sol had heard about him, and I got to admit that I felt good when he looked at me the way he did. He thought that I was really something, and I guess that I felt like I was, too. When I was all done talking, Sol just leaned back on one elbow and looked at me.

"Well, I be damned," he said.

"Well," I said, "we going to do it then, ain't we?"

"Hell yes, we going to do it. By God."

"All right, then," I said, "tell me about them guys you mentioned way while ago."

CHAPTER TWENTY-NINE

Well, old Sol laid back and he told me a tale. Rather, he told me a couple of tales, and they went something like this:

There was a couple of Indian boys name of Knight. They lived outside of Catoosa. Their old man had been beat to death by a white man, and there had never been any charges filed or even an arrest. The white man was a local fellow, well known and pretty popular, and if the killing of the old man, Knight, had done anything at all to his reputation, it had only made him more popular around Catoosa. Sol ran with those boys and had drank, fought, stole and been in and out of jail with them. The oldest was named Richard. He was medium height but stronger than hell and just a little bit slow-thinking. His little brother was called Butcher. Sol said that they could both be counted on when the going got tough.

Another boy that ran with this bunch was a half-breed named French Smith. French's old man made whiskey for a living, and of course French and his brother Dutch helped in the family business, sort of like I helped my old man run the store, I guess. Anyhow, according to Sol, a few months back, Dutch Smith had been going to make the rounds with a wagonload of whiskey. Somehow or other, one of those damn Fort Smith deputies had got wind of Dutch's route. He had him a pocketful of those whiskey warrants. That's what we called them. Really, they were John Doe warrants, which the deputies carried around with them all the time, so they could just arrest anybody they felt like at just any time, and mostly they used them to arrest bootleggers, or at least people they claimed were bootleggers, and most usually, they were Indians.

Well, it happened that this particular Indian was an honest-to-God bootlegger, and this damn lawman, whose name was Ivey, had got wind of his route, and he burned a trail to intercept bootlegger and goods and all at one time. Ivey had laid for Dutch alongside the trail and then held him up with a rifle when he came driving up. He had ordered Dutch to get out of the wagon, and Dutch had started to do it, but when he did, he turned his body slightly to the right, putting his right hand down to lean on the seat. Just then, Ivey had blown him away with two quick rifle shots. His story was that Dutch had been reaching for a shotgun that was lying down under the wagon seat, but Sol said that there had never been a shotgun down there. Ivey had just made a stupid mistake and had to cover it with that story.

Now it seemed as if each one of us had reason to hate the white man, or at least, to hate the white man's law as it was applied to Indians. I never could be convinced that the United States had any right to hold us Indians to its own law. I always remembered the way Henry had talked back when I was a kid, how he had told me and Mose about the Cherokee Nation and having our own government and our own laws and all like that. And then the U.S. government had just took it all away. I couldn't see as how they had any right to do that, so, in a way, I felt like it was right for me to break the white man's law, because, you see, the white man's law was wrong. It didn't, by rights, apply to me or to any other Indian.

I kind of said that to Sol, and he kind of agreed with me, although I didn't feel like he quite really understood what I was trying to get at, but the long and the short of it was that I told Sol that those boys sounded all right to me, especially since he had given them his own personal recommendation and all, so I said that we had ought to get ahold of them, and we agreed and shook hands on it.

CHAPTER THIRTY

I think that it was because of Mose, that is to say, because of the fact that I had been with Mose while he was on the scout, that I sort of took over our gang. It was never really spoke, but Sol just sort of looked toward me, and the others fell in line with him. Right after we all got together, we got to talking about where and how we ought to get started, what kind of job to pull off to get us off on the right foot, so to speak. Actually, I wasn't taking part in this discussion. I was just listening to it and thinking. A couple of stores were suggested and a bank, and one of the Knight boys wanted to rob the little stage that run between Tahlequah and Fort Gibson, but I wasn't thinking about robbery right then. I had got to thinking about Mose, and I know that it's kind of crazy, but I had got to thinking that all the troubles the Cherokees had was the fault of old Moss Berman. In my own mind, I had laid all our problems on his head. I know that's not right, and I guess that I really knew it even then. But I was thinking like that. Moss Berman had killed Mose, and not just Mose but a whole lot of other Indians, making use of those damned whiskey warrants. I got to feeling like if old Berman was dead that things'd get better. And I got to thinking that if nobody else was going to do it, that, well, maybe it was up to me. I know it sounds cold, and I know it sounds wrong, but I felt like it had to be done. I felt like I had to do it. It was up to me. Whether or not they knew it, there was a whole lot of Cherokees and other Indian people depending on me just at that time. Well, you can think that I'm crazy, but that's the way I was feeling.

I had been kind of off to myself, but I came back to the same world everybody else was in, and I heard somebody say something again about that Tahlequah to Fort Gibson stage.

"We ain't going to rob nothing," I said.

They all looked at me and got kind of quiet.

"You changing your mind about this outlaw business now, Charlie?" said Sol.

"No," I said. "Hell, no. I ain't changing my mind on nothing. What I mean is, we ain't going to start off with no robbery. We ain't a bunch of outlaws. They'll call us that, but we ain't. We ain't outlaws, because we ain't white men. If we was white men breaking white men's laws, then we'd be outlaws. But we ain't. We're Indians. They ain't our laws we're fixing to break. They're white men's laws, and the white men are out here in Indian country, trying to make us live by their laws. So we ain't outlaws. Damn it, do you know what I'm saying?"

I looked around the room. French just kind of shrugged his shoulders. Butcher was looking at me like he was waiting for me to finish what I had to say, and Richard was squinting at me real hard. I don't think that any of them had any idea what I was talking about. Richard looked like he was working his brain real hard to try to figure it out. Solomon walked over to me.

"You got the reins, boy," he said. "Where we going?"

"What I'm trying to tell you is that this is war. We ain't no damned outlaws. We're going to war. And we're going to start by killing a federal lawman."

CHAPTER THIRTY-ONE

Well, it took us a little while, but we went to Fort Smith, and we found out where Moss Berman lived. We found out that he had a wife, but they had no kids. We watched him for a few days, and we made our plans. Then one morning, we got ourselves up real early, before sunup, and we went out to his house. It was outside of town just enough for what I had in mind. There were some woods about a hundred yards from the house, and that's where we were. Between us and the house was a big open field. When I was ready, I just reached out and put my hand on French's shoulder. He turned and looked me in the eyes.

"Go on," I said.

French gripped his rifle and looked over at Butcher.

"Let's go," he said.

The two of them started running across the field toward Berman's house. They got up into the yard and took off in different directions, stopping at opposite corners of the hedgerow that ran around the yard. Then they aimed their rifles at the front porch. I saw they were ready, and I nodded at Richard and Sol. Sol fired his rifle into the air, and Richard did the same after him, then commenced to hollering.

"Whoooop. Woooooo ha."

He and Sol sent a few more shots into the air. Then a light came on inside the house. Sol and Richard whooped and shot some more. Then Berman's door came flying open, and out he came onto the front porch. He was barefoot and had on just his trousers. His suspenders were hanging loose. He had a rifle. He went out to the edge of the porch, and he was really looking out into the dark. We just sat quiet. Then French, who was off to Berman's right side, behind the hedgerow, started his part.

"Mr. Berman?" he said in a soft voice.

Berman jerked that rifle up to ready, but he didn't see French, nor anything else. Butcher raised up then and squeezed off a round, which hit Berman in the shoulder, spinning him around. Just then Berman's old lady came out the front door, and she began to scream. Butcher fired a second shot, this one dead-center into Berman's chest. The force of the shot sent the marshal backward, crashing into the wall beside his own doorway. Then he just slid down and turned into a pile of dead meat at his wife's feet. She just kept standing there and screaming.

I walked out into the open field. I was carrying a bow and one arrow. The arrow had a note tied to it that read, "This is for Mose Pathkiller." I nocked the arrow, drew back the string and let fly, and it stuck in the wall just above Berman's body and beside his hysterical wife. Butcher and French rejoined us at the edge of the woods just then, and we all turned and went back into the trees and headed west. And I felt good.

CHAPTER THIRTY-TWO

Well, we had started out like I wanted to, and we did need some supplies, so I decided that we could go on and rob us a store the way the guys had wanted to in the first place. We went all the way over to the country store outside of Okmulgee in the Creek Nation. Sol said that he knew the white man that ran the store and told me that he made his money by cheating the Indians that lived around there. That was good enough for me. We came into the store just as Harper (that was the man's name) had set down in the back to eat his dinner. He had a little bell tied over the door, and it jingled when we went in. I heard him say, "Damn."

He came on out front then, and when he saw us, all five of us, he stopped for just a second, and he looked scared. We all had our rifles in our hands. He backed up a little.

"Uh, just a minute," he said.

Then he kind of halfway opened the back door, which led out to what I guessed was his living quarters. He talked low, but I could understand his words.

"Emma," he said.

I figured that must be his wife.

"Keep quiet. Stay back here and keep this door shut," he told her.

He shut the door and came walking out toward us.

"Hello, boys. What can I do for you?"

"We'd like to look at some handguns," I said.

"Uh, yes. Uh, handguns. Right over here," he said. His voice was quavering.

He walked around behind the counter and reached under it. Then he brought out a pistol from under there, and he laid it real slow and careful up on the counter. His hand was shaking. I thought about

Daddy in his store, and I wondered if he would be acting just this way if it was happening to him. Then I wondered about myself when I was a storekeeper, and how I might have acted if I'd have got robbed at gunpoint. Then I kind of laughed.

"This particular model . . ."

"Never mind the sales talk," I said. "You got four more like it?"

About that time, French must have lost his patience, because he just jumped up and over that counter, and in the process he knocked over some glass jars of stuff that were sitting up there.

"I bet he's got them back here," he said.

He pushed Harper aside and bent over to rummage around the shelves under the counter. Harper grabbed his arm.

"Now wait a minute," he said.

French came up in a hurry and gave Harper a hard shove that threw him backward into the wall shelves and knocked some junk down off them. At the same time, the other four of us raised our rifles and held them aimed at Harper's chest. He stayed put, right up against the shelves where French had shoved him. French came up with the four handguns to add to the one Harper had brought out, and each of us took one and stuck it in our waistbands. Then we got us a mess of shells for the revolvers as well as some for our rifles, and we went around and found us some new shirts and stuff like that to wear. We got some food, too. We had our wits about us enough to remember that. And Sol, he just sort of tore the place up, knocking tables over and that sort of thing. Richard found some whiskey back under the counter, and he took that. One time Harper started to complain, and Butcher started to shoot the floor real close to his feet. Harper kind of danced around, and the guys got a good laugh out of that. When I thought we had everything we needed and was tired of watching the others torment Harper, I hollered out to them.

"Come on," I said. "Let's get the hell out of here."

We went out and mounted up. As we took off, Richard was trying to drink out of his jug while riding, and he had his arms so full of bright-colored shirts and stuff that he was dropping them behind him as he rode. Somehow I didn't feel right. "He's a white man," I told myself, "and he's robbing Indians right here in Indian country. To hell with him. At least we let him live."

CHAPTER THIRTY-THREE

Solomon Web had himself a place out in the woods in the Creek
Nation where he hung out, and that's where we headed. Along the
way, we passed around the jug that Richard had brought. Going down
the road, we saw a wagon coming toward us. The road was narrow, and
we five were riding along abreast, so the wagon came to a halt. We rode
on up close to it. There was a white man driving it, and a little kid
sitting on the wagon seat beside him. We looked pretty ragged, I know,
and I could see that the white man was nervous.

"Howdy, gents," he said.

None of us said anything.

"We'll just set here and let you'ns pass along first," he said.

We still didn't say anything.

"Well, what's wrong? You'ns want something? We ain't got no
money."

Butcher pulled out his pistol, and then Richard did the same.

"Well," said the white man, "hardly none. You can have what we
got. Here, take it. Take it all. Just . . ."

"Just what?" said Butcher.

"Don't shoot us. Please."

He was really scared, and so was the little boy. The boy was hanging
on to the man's arm, and the man was holding out a handful of pocket
change for us to take. Butcher laughed.

"Let my boy go, anyhow. Will you? He's just a boy."

"Shut up that goddamn whining, you white son of a bitch," said
Butcher.

"Yeah," said Richard. "Shut up. We ought to kill you just for the hell
of it."

Sol rode his horse up to the wagon bed and looked in it.

"They ain't got nothing we want," he said.

"Let's go," I said. I was starting to feel sick.

"Wait a minute," said Butcher.

Sol rode over to Butcher and reached out and took ahold of his gun, kind of pushing it down. He was looking straight into Butcher's eyes.

"We better go on, Butcher," he said. "These folks ain't got nothing we want, and we ain't got no call to hurt them."

Butcher stared at Sol for a few seconds. Then he laughed again and kicked his horse and rode on past the wagon. The rest of us followed. When we got past the wagon, the white man started it up, slowly. Then Butcher pulled his gun out again and turned his horse. I was reaching for mine, and I guess I would have shot Butcher, but all he did was he aimed it up in the air and shot five shots off. Richard, like he always did, did the same thing as his brother, and that white man really whipped up his horses and took off down that road. Butcher and Richard laughed most nearly the rest of the way to Sol's place, and when we finally got there I made some excuse to wander off in the woods by myself, and I puked my guts out. Then I went on back to the others and helped to finish off that jug, and we all got drunk and just laid out all that night and all the next day, none of us worth a good goddamn.

CHAPTER THIRTY-FOUR

When we had recovered from the whiskey, we decided to get back to business, and the subject of the stage from Tahlequah to Fort Gibson came up again. This time I agreed with the idea, mainly because I didn't have any better idea of my own, but also because I figured that if I didn't go along some with these crazy bastards that they would all split out on me. I wondered if I maybe wouldn't be better off without them, but they were Indian, and it was war, and once again I didn't have any other ideas. So I decided to go along with the plan to rob the stage. We rode close to Tahlequah on the way, and we happened by the old school where me and Mose had gone. Everybody was outside playing ball, and it didn't look much different from the days when me and Mose were there. Most of the boys were bigger than the teacher. Then I saw Mr. Franklin out there. The guys with me had started to ride on over close to the school, and I didn't say or do anything to stop them. I just rode along.

As we got up close, Mr. Franklin looked up and saw me.

"Why, Charlie Black," he said. "I heard that you just disappeared. What happened?"

"It's Blackbird, Mr. Franklin," I said. "My daddy calls it just Black, but I decided to use the whole name the way it's supposed to be. Blackbird. How are you?"

"Well," said Mr. Franklin, "I'm just fine, but what about you? What's going on?"

"Oh," I said, "nothing's going on. I just got sick of the store and everything that went along with it. I guess I just got sick of trying to be a white man."

I turned toward my companions.

"Fellows," I said, "this here's my old schoolteacher. This is Mr. Franklin. Me and Mose used to go to school to him here."

"How do, Mr. Franklin," said Sol, and he reached out his hand to shake. The others each muttered some kind of greeting. Mr. Franklin took Sol's hand and shook it. He looked kind of puzzled, but he didn't press me any more for answers.

"These here's friends of mine," I told him.

"You fixing to play some ball here?" said Butcher.

"Yes, well, it's recess time," said Mr. Franklin, "and we like to see that it's an active period."

"Can we play?" said Richard.

I began to get worried. I didn't want any trouble for Mr. Franklin.

"Hey," I said, "he don't want us playing ball with the school kids. Don't give him no trouble. Let's go."

"No, that's all right," said Mr. Franklin. "We could use some more players. You used to be pretty good, as I recall, Charlie. Why don't you and your friends play a game with us?"

Well, when they got that invitation, Richard and Butcher were off their horses in no time, and French wasn't too far behind. I looked at

Sol, and he kind of shrugged and grinned, so I did, too, and me and him got off our horses. Once we had chosen up sides, me and Sol found ourselves on a team with a gang of school kids, and the other team was the same but with Butcher and French. Richard had got left out, and Mr. Franklin had asked him to be the umpire. That seemed pretty important to Richard, so he agreed. Mr. Franklin tossed a coin, and my team got sent out to the field.

The boy who was pitching for us struck out the first batter. The second one up got a single on us. The third was another strikeout. The fourth one up hit a ground ball that went right past me in center field.

"Get it, Charlie," yelled Sol, and some other voices were also hollering things at me. I went running after it, but it turned into a double, so they had two men on base.

The fifth batter got up, and, after two strikes and one ball, hit a high fly out over right field. Sol picked it off real neat and tossed it home to retire the side. Well, the next inning went all right until I got up to bat. Then Butcher went running from the field up to the kid on the pitcher's mound.

"Hey, kid, let me pitch to him. Okay?"

"Aw, I don't know."

"Hey, teacher. It's okay if we want to change pitchers, ain't it?"

"Yes," said Mr. Franklin, "it's all right."

I think that Mr. Franklin had begun to see that I was with a kind of rough crowd, and he figured that he hadn't ought to do anything to make any of them mad or anything like that.

"Come on, kid," said Butcher. "Just this one batter. Then I'll change back with you."

"Well, all right."

Butcher stepped up on the mound and grinned at me. Then he really wound that ball up and let it fly.

"Ball one," said Richard.

"What do you mean?" yelled Butcher.

"Play ball," said Richard, as the catcher tossed the ball back.

Butcher did another one of his fancy wind-ups and let fly another at me. Richard called that one a strike. The next one was another ball, and the next one.

"Ball three," said Richard.

"God damn it, Richard," said Butcher. "That was a strike."

As he said that, Butcher was headed in for Richard.

"It was a ball, you dumb shit," said Richard.

"You're as blind as a bat."

A kid out in left field yelled at them.

"Hey, come on. You're holding up the game."

"Shit," said Butcher, but he headed back for the mound.

He pitched me another one.

"Strike two," called Richard.

"Damn," I said.

"Not you, too," said Richard. "Hell, nobody likes the umpire."

Butcher got the ball back, and he really looked at me. He was mad, and I could tell that he really wanted to strike me out. He wanted to really burn one through there. I got myself ready, and in spite of myself I was feeling, if not as mad as him, at least as determined. I wanted to knock that damn thing right through his teeth. It got quiet. Butcher ground the ball against his hip.

"Hey, come on," said one of the kids.

Out of the corner of my eye, I could see Mr. Franklin. He was getting really nervous, and I felt kind of sorry for him, but I thought that I'd get this bat over with before I worried about it. I got set. Butcher wound up again and really put everything he had behind it. I pulled back a bit, but then I changed my mind. I didn't swing.

"Ball four," said Richard. "Take your base."

"You blind bastard," said Butcher, and he was charging for Richard.

"If I'm a bastard, what's that make you?" said Richard. "You're my brother."

"Go to hell," said Butcher, and he hit his brother a solid right to the jaw. Richard staggered back a couple of steps, then ducked his head and ran it right into Butcher's guts, and everyone on both teams came running up to get a good, close spot to watch from. Richard and Butcher were just locked together and rolling in the dirt. The kids were all yelling. I looked around for Mr. Franklin, and I saw him. He didn't know what to do. He wanted to do something, but he was just sort of fidgeting around. I felt like I had done something awful to him, and I felt like I had to stop it. I pulled the pistol out of my pants and shot it into the air. After they jumped, everybody got real quiet. Richard and Butcher had come apart real fast, and each had drawn his own pistol, and the two of them were sitting there in the dirt, looking dumb as hell, and looking around to see who was shooting at them. Then they saw it was me.

"Let's go, boys," I said. "We've done spoiled the ball game. Besides, we got places to go."

As we rode off, I could see Mr. Franklin staring after me, and I knew that he wanted real bad to talk to me and to find out what I was doing and who these guys were that I was with. I knew that he'd always liked me, and that he meant well, and I wished that I could just stay behind and have a nice long talk with him. But I also knew that it wouldn't have done any good. Mose had talked with him, had believed in him, and look where it led for Mose. Then I begun to think of all the times me and Mose had around that old school, and I wished that it was back then again, and I was glad that we were riding, because I could feel the tears starting to come into my eyes, and I sure didn't want my gang to see that.

CHAPTER THIRTY-FIVE

It was about ten o'clock in the morning when that stage came rolling along the road to where we were laid up in the brush waiting for it. It was heading west. That is, it was on its way to Fort Gibson from Tahlequah. It was a hot day, and the road was dusty. It was a narrow, winding road, too, and when that stage started to get close, we just stepped out and lined up across the road with our guns out. When the driver saw us there, he hauled back on the reins right snappy-like.

"Whoa," he said. "Whoa up."

At the same time, he pulled back the brake handle, and that stage came to a halt right there in front of us. Somebody inside hollered up at him.

"What's going on here now?" said the voice. "What are you stopping here for?"

About then, the man who was doing the hollering started out the door. He was fat and short, and he had on a dark suit and a derby hat. He came puffing out that door, but he had only got halfway when he saw us. He stopped just like that.

"Toss down your guns," I said to the driver.

He did it.

"Sol," I said, "get them passengers out."

Sol went on over to the stage door. The little fat man was still there, half in and half out.

"Well, come on," said Sol.

The fat man got on out.

"You got a gun?" said Sol.

"N-no," said the fat man. "No."

"Well," said Sol, "I'll just check to be sure."

Sol felt around under the man's coat, and then he pushed him over to one side.

"All right," he said, "the rest of you all come on out of there."

A young couple got out, the man white and the woman Indian, dressed in their Sunday best. Then two young men, white men, got out, and finally an old Indian woman. Sol took some guns off the two young men and tossed them in the dirt. French started to go through the pockets of the fat man. He got a gold watch and eighty-six dollars. Butcher took the old woman's handbag and started to look inside it.

"Give it back," I said.

"What?"

"I said, 'Give it back.' "

Butcher looked at me. Then he looked at the woman, and I guess then he remembered or realized what was in my head. He gave the woman back her handbag. While this was going on, Richard had gone over to the young couple. I wasn't watching him like I should have been, because he must have done something to that young Indian woman. Anyhow, her husband all of a sudden got brave and shoved Richard.

"You keep your hands off her," he said.

Richard staggered back a few steps, and while he was fumbling around like that, he was in between the other two white boys and the rest of us. One of them grabbed up one of the guns from the road and fired a shot that knocked Richard's hat off his head. Richard hollered like he'd been killed and made a dive for the brush off the side of the road. I jumped for cover too, and then it got real quiet. I waited a bit, and then I peeked out real slow and easy, and what I saw was that the road was deserted. The coach was setting there, but there weren't no human beings in sight. Whenever that shot was fired, I guess, everybody jumped for the nearest cover, so there we were. Everybody hiding from everybody else. Nobody knowing where nobody else was.

All of a sudden I heard a rustling and a shot, and I looked out as careful as ever I could, and I seen old Sol plowing through the brush like an old bull. He was headed in the general direction of where we had left our horses. I figured that made sense. I didn't know where anybody else was at, and anyhow, they were each most likely to do the same thing as Sol had done as soon as they saw their chance, so I thought I might as well do the same. The job was messed up, and I didn't have any reason to want to see any of those people dead, so I decided that I'd get the hell out of there myself. I made my way through the brush and out on the other side, where I saw that there were only two horses left. They were mine and Richard's. I guessed that the others had all done took out. I mounted up and headed east, but I had just got going when I heard a woman hollering. There was a dry wash just on the edge of the woods which I had come through to get to my horse, and I rode over to its edge. There I found Richard. He had the young woman that had been on the stage with her husband. The gal was lying on her back in the soft dirt of the wash, and Richard was standing over her with a pistol in his hand. She was kind of reluctantly pulling up her skirts, while Richard was fumbling with his breeches. I eased my horse back away from the edge of the wash. Neither one of them had seen me.

"God damn him," I said to myself. "That's an Indian woman."

But I didn't want to start trouble in the ranks, and I didn't want to shoot the bastard. I got off my horse and went back to the edge of the wash on foot, carrying my rifle along with me. I took real careful aim, and I fired a shot into the dirt just off to Richard's left. Richard jumped backward at the shot, and when he did, he tripped over his breeches, which had just dropped down to around his ankles. He fell on his bare ass, and I almost laughed out loud, as mad as I was. Then I shot again, and Richard scrambled to his feet. He was trying to pull up his pants and run at the same time. He fell two more times while I watched, and to keep him hopping, I fired two more shots. When the gal saw what was happening, she got up and took off back through the woods in the direction of the road and the stage. With her running that direction, and Richard running the opposite direction, toward his horse, I figured that she was safe enough, so I got back to my horse and took off before Richard could get a chance to see that it was me who had messed up his fun.

On down the trail a ways, we all got back together, and it wasn't long before everybody got over being mad about what a mess we had made and began to see the humor in it. We all had a good laugh over the whole crazy episode, but especially over Richard, who was the last one to join us and who showed up riding bare-assed in the saddle, his trousers stringing along beside him, hanging off one foot.

CHAPTER THIRTY-SIX

French Smith wanted to go visit his folks and leave them some of the few dollars we had from our feeble attempts at robbery. We all decided to go along with him for the ride, and when he had done with his visit, we would all go about our business, whatever that might be. So we rode to the Smiths' home. We weren't hardly expecting what we found there, though.

The old man looked like he had really got a going-over from somebody, and French's mama had a couple of bruises on her face. French got all excited, and he asked them what the hell had happened, but he wouldn't hardly shut up long enough to let them answer. They finally convinced him that they were all right, and got him to introduce his friends to them, and they gave us all some corn bread and coffee, and then they told us what had happened to them.

"A lawman came here looking for you," the old man said to French.

"For me?" said French.

"For you and your friends here, I guess. He said that you been running with a gang of outlaws, and he wanted to know where to find you. He talked to your mama first, and you know her English ain't so good. Well, when I come out the door, he almost drawed on me. I guess maybe he thought it might be you coming out. Well, he talked real big and tough, you know. Cussing and threatening. That kind of talk. I told him that I ain't seen you for some time, and I don't know where you're at, or who you're with, or nothing. Then he pulled out his pistol and knocked me around with it. Your mama tried to stop him a couple of times, and he knocked her around, too. But we never told him nothing. Of course, we never knowed nothing to tell him, really."

"God damn it," said French.

"Them son of a bitches," said Sol. "They think they can do any damn thing they want to do and get away with it."

"Papa," said French, "do you know who he was?"

The old man looked at the floor, and he looked sad and, I thought, a little ashamed.

"Did you ever see him before, Papa?"

"I seen him," said the old man. "I seen him right after he killed your brother."

"Ivey," said French. "It was Ivey? Goddamn."

I hadn't said a word since we'd been there. I'd just been setting and taking it all in. But when I heard that name, and I remembered the story of what had happened to French's older brother, I made a decision right there. I set down my coffee cup and stood up from my place at the table.

"Fellows," I said, "I think that we just got our next job all laid out for us."

Richard looked up at me.

"We going to kill him, Charlie?" he asked.

"Naw," I said. "Hell, no. We ain't going to kill him."

CHAPTER THIRTY-SEVEN

Well, we found out just when Ivey had been there and which direction
he had headed off in, and we visited a couple of the Smiths' neighbors
not far away to find out if they could help us any. Sure enough, Ivey
had stopped in to see them, too. We found out that he not only had
French's name, but he had Sol's and the Knights'. I was the only one
whose name he didn't have. I imagined that was because we had been
operating so much in the Creek Nation, where people didn't know me
but knew the others. He didn't know where Sol lived, but he knew
where the Smiths and the Knights lived, so we figured he was headed
for the Knights' place. We figured out which way he was probably
going, and Butcher told us that he knew a way we could get ahead of
him and probably cut him off. So we hurried cross-country and made
our way to a little creek that Butcher figured Ivey would be showing up
at before too much longer. We tied our horses up a good ways down the
creek from where Ivey would be crossing, and then we found ourselves
a good spot from which we could hide and watch, and we just settled
down right there.

We had to wait quite a while, but it turned out that Butcher had
figured it right, for Ivey came riding down the trail leading to the creek
crossing. He was riding along real leisurely-like. When he came to the
creek, he stopped and got off his horse. It was a hot day, and we had
been hoping that he'd stop to wet his whistle in the creek. That's just
what he had in mind, too. He let his horse drink, and he took off his
hat and pulled a red bandanna out of his hip pocket to wipe his face off
with. He got down on his knees beside the creek and dipped that
bandanna in the water. Then he just kind of leaned back until he rolled
over on his back and just stretched out on the ground, and he put that

bandanna right over his face. Just covered his whole face with that wet rag and lay there.

He must have been real surprised to have his rest interrupted the way it was, by the noise of a revolver hammer being drawn back. I guess there ain't no sound quite like it. Anyhow, he tore that bandanna from off his face with his left hand and his right was reaching for his gun, but Richard Knight, who was holding a rifle, fired a shot—I don't know what he meant for it to do, but it tore the thumb off Ivey's right hand. Ivey screamed and grabbed his right hand with his left. Blood was just running.

Butcher walked over to Ivey, who had rolled over kind of on his right side, and when Ivey looked up a little at him, he swung out and down with his right arm, catching Ivey on the side of his head with the back of his hand. Ivey had been thrown over on his left side then, and Richard just reached down and took his gun off him. Then he hauled off and pitched the gun into the creek.

I looked at French Smith, and I could see the hate in his eyes.

"It's your move, French," I said.

French wasn't even holding a gun in his hands, and he started toward Ivey. Ivey started sort of scooching himself backward over the rocks, reaching out behind him with his good hand, trying to get up to his feet.

"N-now wait a minute," he was saying, but just about then, French smashed a fist into the side of his face, and the way it sounded, I'm sure that at least one tooth was loosened.

"I'm the law," Ivey shouted out.

I guess he thought that he could slow us down by giving us that bit of information, but we already knew that and, in fact, that was the reason we were doing what we were doing. So instead of backing off, French pulled out his pistol and began to whack around on Ivey's head some. He hit him three or four times, making some ugly cuts and gashes on his head, and then he hauled back like he was fixing to deal the death blow. He had that pistol raised up real high above his head, and he was just about to bring it down on Ivey's noggin. I didn't much give a damn what he did, but Sol must have.

"French, hold on," he said.

French paused, but he still held that gun up over his head, and he was still looking down at Ivey.

"That's too easy, boy," said Sol. "It don't hurt near as long that way."

Ivey had managed to get himself up into a squatting position, and while he was watching French real close and taking everything in, he was trying to stand on up. He had managed to get to about a half-standing position. French seemed like Sol had got to him, and he let his pistol hang down by his side and turned to start to walk away from Ivey. Then he changed his mind right quick, turned back around and give Ivey a quick kick to the balls. Richard, Butcher and Sol had all moved up close by then, and they was all kind of circled around Ivey, who was lying in the rocks and whimpering. I was hanging back and just watching.

I didn't have any use for Ivey. I didn't like the things that he stood for, and I didn't like the things I knew about that he had done. I'd have been glad to have put a bullet in him from the front or back, even from ambush, with no warning or anything. I wouldn't have give a damn. But I didn't really have any stomach for this kind of tormenting of a man. Of course, it was French's brother that Ivey had killed, and it was French's folks that he had beat on. So I figured that it was really French's business and not mine. Maybe if it had been my family, maybe I'd have felt the same way. Maybe. I don't know. But still yet, I didn't have any stomach for it, and I wished that they would just get it over with and done.

"Say," I heard Butcher say, "them's pretty fancy boots he's got on, i'n'it? They look to be about your size, French."

French reached down and pulled Ivey's boots off his feet, jerking around on them real rough. Ivey was still hurting bad, and that didn't help him none at all. He moaned and groaned, but he couldn't do anything else. When French had got the boots, Sol reached down and pulled Ivey to his feet by his shirtfront. He held him up by his shirt while he slapped his face a few times, talking to him all the while.

"You like to slap old folks around, i'n'it? You a goddamn dog is what you are. A damn dog."

Ivey's feet were slipping on the sharp rocks, but Sol wouldn't let him fall down. I'd had about all of that stuff that I could take. I walked over to Ivey and took him out of Sol's hands.

"A dog, huh?" I said. "He looks like a whipped dog to me. Maybe you need a drink. Yeah? Come on down here to the creek and get yourself a drink."

I half-dragged Ivey down to the edge of the creek, and then I gave him a shove, so that he fell headlong into the creek. He lifted himself up on his hands and looked back at me. I never saw a grown man look so pitiful.

"Go on," I said. "Drink. Like a dog."

Richard Knight caught on and started laughing.

"Drink like a dog," he said. "Drink like a dog."

Ivey stuck his face down in the creek and lapped at some water. He looked back over his shoulder at me. Then he looked at the others.

"Now get on out of here," I said.

Ivey started to straighten up. He was looking toward his horse.

"That way," I said, and I pointed up the creek.

Ivey backed slowly into the creek. He started to try walking in the knee-deep water, his sock feet slipping on the sharp rocks.

"Like a dog," said Richard. "Like a dog."

Ivey dropped to his hands and knees and began crawling upstream. Richard laughed aloud, and he was joined by Butcher and Sol. French was still too mad to find much humor in the situation, and I was a little surprised that he let me get away with what I had done, but he just stood there and watched Ivey crawling away.

CHAPTER THIRTY-EIGHT

What was happening to me was something I never expected to happen, but I was beginning to get kind of sick of the whole mess. I mean, it wasn't like what I thought it was going to be like. It wasn't the way I felt like it ought to be. And the main thing, I guess, is that it wasn't really anything like what it had been like with Mose. I ain't exactly sure what it was about it that bothered me. I had made the choice. I had decided for myself that I could best carry on for Mose by taking to the outlaw trail, except that all the victims of my outlawry would only be whites. It was to be a kind of a war. And I guess that's what it was that was wrong. It didn't feel like a war. It didn't feel anything at all like a war. It had felt that way with Mose.

Why, Mose's old man had been shot up, and his brother had been killed, and all for nothing. Mose had reasons, and I guess that I had my reasons, too, because Mose was the best friend that I ever had, and because his family was Cherokee, and I'm Cherokee. And, of course, the Cherokees were still getting pushed around by the white man, or by the United States government, and those guys I was with, they had their reasons too, just like Mose had his and I had mine. And it should have been the same, but it wasn't. I know that part of the reason was that we were stealing money. And then I had to stop them from stealing from Indians, and I'd had to stop Richard Knight from raping that Indian girl. We had done in a couple of lawmen who needed doing in, and I felt good about that, but I guess that in order to do the things that I felt like we ought to be doing, I was having to go along with some other things that I didn't believe in, things that I didn't like doing and that I felt bad about. So what it all came up to was that I was really the only one of the bunch that felt like I did. They weren't really with me. And then, too, when I had been with Mose, I had been following him. He had been the leader. And with this bunch, I was sort of the leader, and it wasn't the same. And I began to realize that it wouldn't ever be the same, and I was beginning to try to think of a way to get myself loose from the whole damn mess.

The only problem I had was that I didn't know what else to do. I knew that I couldn't ever go back home. Oh, Velma would probably have taken me back, if I had come crawling in and whined around and said that I was sorry and all like that. She'd have given me hell about it, and I'd have had to put up with it probably for the rest of my life, but she'd have took me back. And I imagine that Daddy would even have took me back into the store with him. In fact, I was legal half-owner. But I knew that I'd be miserable if I went back to either one of those two situations. I had been there before, and I had hated it, and that was why I was where I was, so I knew that I would never go back to that kind of life.

There was also the problem that I didn't really know whether or not my activities were known to the law, or to anybody else. They could have been, but I didn't know it for sure. All we knew for sure was that Sol and French and the Knights had all been identified. But I felt like there was a pretty fair chance that they knew about me, too. At least, I felt like there was a good enough chance that I wasn't going to be stupid enough to take a chance on going back where folks knew me and stick my own neck in a noose.

So that was the kind of problems I was wrestling with. I wanted out of what I was into, but I couldn't figure out where else to go.

CHAPTER THIRTY-NINE

Well, when we drove old Ivey off down the creek, we didn't really have any plans concerning what we wanted to do next, and the boys were getting just a little itchy for some kind of action. Only the kind of action they wanted wasn't at all the kind that I had in my mind. They were thinking of fun. They were wanting to do some serious drinking, and then there was Richard, whose fun in the dry wash I had interrupted, and I reckon I knew what was on his mind.

Anyhow, there was a place over on Fourteen Mile Creek called the Halfway House, where any of that could be had, and that's where they decided they wanted to go. I went along with it, just because I didn't have any other ideas in my head for right then, so we rode on over there. It was just about fourteen miles away from Tahlequah, which may or may not be where the creek got its name, and I remember that I was just a little nervous about getting so close to home again, but I didn't say anything about it. There was a woman named Maggie something-or-other who ran the place. They said that she was Cherokee, but if she was, she was a breed, because she looked like a white woman to me. And they said that she was married to a lawman, but that they were separated, and that he never came around out there. I figured that

I'd just get drunk, and I hoped that by the time I sobered up, that they'd all had their fun and be ready to go. That ain't exactly the way things worked out.

CHAPTER FORTY

When we arrived at the Halfway House, it was well after dark, and we were all pretty much wore out, so all we did was we just got us some beds, and we were all snoozing away in no time at all. We slept most of the next morning away, too, but even so, when we did get up, Maggie cooked us all some bacon and eggs, and we must have drunk up at least two gallons of coffee.

Well, I hadn't even finished eating my breakfast when old Richard got started. I guess he still had his problem, never having got it took care of, largely due to my interference, which he still didn't know about. Anyhow, Richard was trying his damnedest to get Maggie to go back in the back room with him where the beds were.

"I don't feel like it right now," she was telling him. "Besides that, I don't need no money bad enough to have to do that. I run a honest place here, and I got my own money. I don't need none of yours. Not like that, anyhow. I'll take your money for bed and board, and that's it."

"Aw, come on, Maggie," Richard said. "Come on. It ain't like you ain't done it before. And money don't last forever. You'll need more of it soon enough. Come on."

He was tugging on Maggie, standing behind her with one hand on each of her skinny shoulders. She wasn't struggling with him either, just kind of standing there in the middle of the room. Her weight was about equal on both feet, so that whenever Richard pulled on her, her body just kind of sagged a little bit in whatever direction he was pulling. I thought that she seemed like wet dough. Her feet never moved,

and she just had a sort of blank expression on her face. I remember
thinking that Richard must really be bad off to want to crawl under the
sheets with that dishwater-looking white woman, anyhow. Her hair was
kind of mousy-colored, and it was wet from sweat, and stringy. Her face
was tight-looking, and her lips were so thin that she didn't hardly have
no lips at all. And she was so skinny that her old dress, which had been
washed so many times that it didn't have any color left in it at all, just
looked like it was hanging on a hook or something. Goddamn, I
thought, he must really be bad off, and I glanced over at him, and I
could see visible evidence that he was really getting excited. I tried to
ignore them and went on back to eating my breakfast.

"Come on," said Richard, and I saw him let his hands slide down
from her shoulders to the front of her dress, where her breasts would
have been if she'd had any, and he started squeezing on her there, and
he gave her a sloppy kiss on the side of her neck just below the ear. All
she did was she just kind of sagged a little in the opposite direction.
Some strings of her sweaty hair stuck to Richard's lips.

"Come on."

"I ain't going to do it," she said. "I sure ain't going to do it right
now, in the middle of the day like this. It ain't decent."

"Oh, come on."

"No, I said. It ain't decent, and I ain't going to do it. Not now."

Richard looked like a kid whose mama had just slapped his hands.

"A little later?" he said. "After a while then?"

"I ain't going to say one way or the other, except to say that I sure
ain't going to do it in the middle of the day."

"Tonight, after dark, then. Okay?"

"I ain't saying. I got to go to town to take care of some business, and
I'll be gone most of the day. If you want to stay here, it's all right. You
know where everything is, and you know what it costs. If you decide to
leave before I get back, just leave me my money for it."

"We ain't going nowhere until you get back," said Richard. "I got
plans for when you get back."

"Yeah? Well, we'll see about that."

Maggie picked up a few things and left for town. As she shut the
door behind herself, Richard began pacing back and forth across the
room.

"Goddamn," he said.

Butcher laughed out loud.

"You poor son of a bitch," he said.

"Oh yeah?" said Richard. "If I'm a son of a bitch, what the hell does that make you? You're my brother."

"You ain't going to get none of that," said Butcher, ignoring the question, "so you might just as well forget about it. You dumb ass."

Richard had grabbed Butcher by the shirtfront and thrown him on the floor before Butcher knew what was happening. And before Butcher could scramble back up onto his feet, Richard was on top of him.

"Get him off," I said to Solomon.

Sol walked up behind Richard and pulled him off his brother.

"You keep the hell out of this," said Richard.

"Hold on, damn it," I said, and I raised my voice enough to really get their attention. "No use in tearing this place up. If you two want to fight, why don't you go on outside to kill each other? I can't see fighting over that skinny bitch anyhow."

"Who's fighting over her?" said Butcher. "Hell, I wasn't fighting over her. I don't fight over no woman."

"Well, I wasn't fighting over Maggie," said Richard.

"What the hell did you jump me for then?"

"Well, I . . ."

"Goddamn," I said. "You don't even know."

I got up and found a bottle of whiskey, and I took it with me outside and down to the creek, where I set myself down under a nice shade tree and commenced to get drunk. Pretty soon, I got some woozy, and then I dropped off to sleep. I don't know what the others did to pass away the afternoon.

CHAPTER FORTY-ONE

When I came to, I had to think for a minute before I could recall where I was at. I was sore from lying on the rocks, and my head was kind of fuzzy from the whiskey. I had a little bit of a headache, and I was hungry as hell, which wasn't too surprising, since the sun was already sort of low in the west. I got up slow and ambled back to the house. On the way in I saw that Maggie's buggy was back, but I didn't see her when I got inside. Butcher and Solomon and French were setting around the table drinking whiskey. I didn't see Richard. I started to ask where Maggie was at, because I wanted something to eat, but before I said anything I heard the voices from the back room. The first voice I heard was Richard's, and while he was talking, he must have been bouncing around on the bed, because I could hear the springs creaking.

"Aw, come on, Maggie," he was saying. "God a'mighty."

For a while I heard sounds that I figured was Maggie getting out of her clothes. Then the bed really began to creak, as if she had jumped right into it, or, what I thought was more likely, he had pulled her onto it or thrown her onto it. I couldn't imagine Maggie showing enough enthusiasm to jump into bed with anybody. Then the sounds started to get pretty obvious all right, and Butcher kind of snickered.

"Is there anything to eat in this goddamned place?" I asked.

Solomon got up and walked over to the cabinet on the wall.

"Yeah," he said. "It ain't nothing to brag about, but it's food."

He opened the cabinet and started to get some stuff out for me, and I heard Richard start to gasp and groan. Sol handed me a knife and a hard loaf of bread on a board. I heard Richard in the other room.

"Oh, Lord God Jesus."

I took the board and walked over to the table. The creaking of the bedsprings suddenly became loud and regular. There were about five or six fast creaks, and then they stopped. I sat down, and I heard Richard moan. I started to cut the bread. Sol sat a cup of coffee on the table in front of me.

"You want this?"

"Maggie," Richard was saying real low, like he didn't want us to hear it, "Maggie, don't you go nowhere. Don't go nowhere, because I can do it again. Just you wait a bit, and I can do it again."

"Yeah, Sol, thanks," I said.

Butcher got up and went to the door leading into the back room. He opened it.

"Hey, goddamn," said Richard. "Get the hell out of here."

"You done had your turn," said Butcher. "Now it's mine."

"Hell, no. I ain't done."

"Be a good boy and run along," said Maggie. "Give somebody else a chance. You can come back after a while. When you're all rested up."

"Aw, hellfire," said Richard.

After a bit of shuffling, Richard came out into the main room. He came straight to the table and got some whiskey. I went back over to the cabinet and found some dried meat. I remember wondering vaguely just exactly what had been dried, but I took a handful and headed for the door. I didn't feel like listening to the sounds from the back room any longer, so I headed back down for the creek. It was dark already by then. I made my way kind of slow back down to the same spot I had used to snooze away the afternoon. I sat back down under the tree and began to gnaw at the dry meat. I was mad. I thought that I was mad at Richard and Butcher, and then I thought that I was mad at Maggie. But then I asked myself how come I should be mad at any of them. I mean, why should I give a damn what any one of them had done or was doing? What I realized, when I had thought about it for a while, made me even madder than before, but then it was at my own self. I was mad at myself, because I realized that I was wanting to go back up there and take my turn with Maggie, too. And the reason that made me mad was that what they were doing up there was disgusting to me. Maggie was a whore, and that disgusted me. Taking turns disgusted me, and finally, Maggie's physical appearance was pretty disgusting to me, too.

"Damn," I said out loud.

I got to wanting some whiskey, and I couldn't get that bottle up on the table out of my mind, so I got up and went back up the hill and into the house. When I opened the door, I saw Solomon, Richard and Butcher setting around the table. French Smith must have been in the back room.

"Shit," I said.

I poured myself a drink.

"Your turn next, Sol?" I said.

Sol laughed.

"No, Charlie," he said, "I done been. Frenchie's the last one. That is, unless you going in."

"No, by God," said Richard. "I'm next. I'm going in there again. It was my idea, and I'm going back."

"Don't worry, Richard," I said. "I'm not going back there."

Sol laughed again.

"What's the matter with you, boy?" he said. "She's hot."

"Yeah," said Butcher. "She ain't nothing like she pretends to be. You get in bed with her, she's a whole different woman. She like to whipped me to death, and she ain't satisfied yet."

"Yeah?" I said. "Well, you go back after Richard then. I'm going down to the creek and get drunk."

I took the bottle off the table, but before I could turn to head for the door, I felt a hand on my shoulder.

"Come on in."

It was Maggie. I looked around just a little by turning my head. She was stark naked.

"I ain't interested," I said.

I said that, but I was lying, and I was afraid that they all knew that I was lying. My heart pounded, and my knees started to shake. Maggie moved up against my back and slipped her hands under my arms and around onto my chest and belly.

"Come on with me," she said.

I didn't know what to say. I wanted to go with her, but I didn't want the others to know about it. I wished to God that they were gone. I wished that I had never said anything, so that it wouldn't have been such a big deal if I had gone on with her. I hated her for what she was doing to me, and I wanted to turn around and knock the shit out of her. But I was afraid to turn around and look at her standing there in

that room with five men and her naked like that. Then she slid her
hands down to my waist and shoved them inside my breeches. I shiv-
ered. Solomon Web laughed.

"Go on ahead, Charlie," he said. "It'll be good for you."

"You won't be sorry," said Maggie. "I'll make it good for you."

"Hell, I can't stand no more of this," said Sol, still laughing, and he
walked to the door and opened it to go outside, but when he did, there
was a loud explosion, and he came flying backward, back into the table
and fell across it. His eyes were wide open, and there was a big red hole
in his chest. Richard and Butcher ran for their guns. Maggie screamed.
Her hands were still inside my pants, and she couldn't pull them loose.
I had started for the door, but I couldn't get there for dragging her
behind me. French was by a window, and he took a quick look outside.

"The laws," he said. "It's the laws."

"Well, shut the goddamn door," I said.

Butcher rolled across the floor and kicked the door shut, just as more
shots were fired from outside. Maggie finally got her hands out of my
breeches and ran screaming for the back room. I got my gun.

"Get the lights out," I said.

Richard did what I said, and once it was dark inside, the shots
stopped. I was quiet.

"Charlie?"

I recognized Butcher's voice.

"Yeah?"

"Sol. Is he . . . ?"

"Deader than hell," I said.

"What now?" said French.

"I don't know," I said. "Just keep down and keep quiet. Let me
think."

It got real quiet again. I couldn't hear a damn thing, inside or out.
Just my own breathing.

"French," I said.

"Huh?"

"Look out that window again. Can you see anything out there?"

"I can't see a goddamn thing."

"Okay," I said. "Butcher, can you get out the back way and get our
horses ready?"

"Hell, yeah."

"Okay, you do that. We'll keep them busy out here. Go on."
Butcher headed for the back door.
"French. Richard," I said. "Shoot out them windows."
"Where do we shoot?"
"I don't give a damn. They're out there somewhere. Just shoot. Keep
them busy."

They started shooting out into the darkness, and as soon as they did,
whoever was out there begun shooting back. At least then we had the
flashes from their shots to aim back at. Butcher had already gone on
outside the back way. And then I heard some shots that sounded like
they came from out back.
"Butcher's in trouble," said Richard.
"You stay where you're at," I said. "I'll go."
I ran for the back door before Richard could give me any argument.
I went through the bedroom, and I saw, out of the corner of my eye as
I ran through, Maggie lying there on top of the bed, still naked, hug-
ging a pillow. As I ran out the back door, I saw the flash from a shot
and saw Butcher fall against the house. I shot at where I had seen the
flash, and I heard a scream. Somebody else shot from somewhere and
hit Butcher in the right hand, knocking his gun away and smashing his
hand up pretty bad. I fired some more shots out into the darkness, not
knowing what I was shooting at, and I grabbed Butcher around the
waist and pulled him back inside through the bedroom door. I could
feel the hot, sticky blood running down his side. I dragged him over to
the bed.
"Watch out," I said to Maggie.
I heaved Butcher onto the bed beside her. She moved away real fast
and sat up on the opposite side of the bed, looking kind of scared and
all huddled up. Butcher was moaning like hell. I could see that he was
hurt bad. I went back into the main room.
"We got to get out of here," I said. "I don't know how, because they
got us surrounded. They're out back and out front. But if we don't
figure some way out of here, Butcher's going to die. He's shot up bad.
They'll get the rest of us, too."
"Who the hell are them guys?" said Richard.
"The laws," said French.
"Hell, I know that, but I mean, where the hell did they come from?
How'd they know we was here?"

All of a sudden the answer came to my mind, but I didn't want to say it. Even though I didn't have any use for her, I don't hold with killing women. But it didn't do any good for me to keep my mouth shut, because I wasn't the only one doing some thinking. It was quiet for just a bit before French spoke up again.

"Maggie," he said. "She went into town. She's married to one of them bastards, too."

"She got the laws on us?" said Richard. "Maggie?"

"Who else?"

"I'm going to blow her goddamn head off."

Richard stood up to make his way to the bedroom, but just as he did, somebody outside decided to fire a few more shots at us, and he hit the floor again.

"Forget about her," I said. "We got more important things to worry about right now."

"Charlie," said French, "how are we going to get out of here?"

"Maybe," I said, "if we go out slow and easy, maybe they won't see us. It's really dark out there. Listen. I'll go out the front door. You go out the back. Give us a little time to get out there, Richard, and then you take your brother and get to the horses. With us out ahead of you, maybe you'll have a better chance of getting him out of here. Forget about us. Just get out of here with him and get him to a doctor. If they can see us when we go out, they'll be busy with us. Sneak through them if you can. Kill them if you run up on them. Every man on his own, once we get outside. Let's go then. Slow and easy. And quiet."

I eased over to the front door and waited, while French and Richard moved into the back room. I could hear Richard moving his brother off the bed and dragging him toward the back door. I thought I heard the back door open, and if I was right, then it ought to have been French going on out. I opened the front door a little. There weren't any shots. I stayed down and kind of crawled outside, and then I just stayed hunched up against the wall there beside the front door for a bit. I guess nobody saw me, because nobody shot at me. When I got to feeling a little more secure, I started working my way out away from the house, toward where I thought they were hiding among the trees. I got to a brushy spot and got myself hid out good and snug. I settled in there for a bit and listened. I couldn't for the life of me figure out where they were at. Then all at once came the sounds of a gunfight and the sound of a horse riding out hard and fast. Richard must have been riding out with Butcher. The gunshots could have been somebody shooting at them, or it could have been French keeping the laws' attention. I hoped that it was French. The shooting stopped, and it got real quiet again. In a little while, I like to jumped out of my skin, when I heard a voice whispering off in the dark, and it sounded right close to me.

"Houston?" it said.

Well, I reckoned that I knew who that was. Houston Rattler was a Cherokee lawman. We were fighting Cherokees. I got all confused about what I was doing and about why I was where I was at and even about who the hell I was. I had naturally assumed that it was federal marshals out there. I was almost sick, and for the first time, I was really scared.

"Yeah?" Houston answered.

"You see anything?"

"Nope."

"What do you think happened back there?"

"Hell, how should I know?"

"Sounded to me like they got away."

"Could be."

"Well, what are we going to do? Sit here in the dark all night or what?"

"You want to stick your fool head up and get it blowed off trying to find out if any of them's still in there?"

They stopped talking, and I just kept still. After a while they started in again.

"Hey, Houston. I think they all got away in the dark."

"I don't know."

"Well, I think they did, and I think that our boys is all gone, too. It's too damn quiet out here."

He didn't get an answer that time. He waited for one, but then he just went on himself.

"I'm heading back. You coming with me?"

"Yeah," said Houston, after a long pause, "let's get out of here."

They began to move out real slow, trying not to give themselves away. I just sat tight and listened. Directly I heard them start to ride off on their horses, which they must have left a good ways off, so that we wouldn't hear them approaching the house when they first came up. The sound was real faint, but I could hear them riding off. I figured they were the only ones in front of the house, because if there had been any more, they would have heard the same thing I did and either stopped them or joined them. So I waited just a bit more to be safe, and then I got up and went around back. It took me a while, because I moved as cautious as before, but pretty soon I found French and two lawmen out back, all dead. The lawmen were Indians, all right.

I thought that the laws were all gone, but to make sure I walked away off down the road and found where they had left their horses. I found two horses for the two dead ones, so I figured I was right. They had all left. I went back to the house to get my few belongings, and I thought that right then in the dark, I would mount up and get going. I didn't know where I would go, but I didn't think that I wanted to hang around there anymore, but I had walked in the house by the back door, and I could just barely see her outline in the dark. There sat Maggie on the edge of the bed right where I had last seen her, and she was still as naked.

CHAPTER FORTY-TWO

I just stood there in the dark room and stared at her outline. She had turned her head and was looking at me, but other than that she hadn't moved.

"Charlie?" she said.

"Yeah," I said. "It's me."

"What happened?"

"It's all over," I said. "At least for right now. There's three dead out there. Maybe more. The rest all took off."

"Light the lamp," she said.

I found it and lit it. I turned it down low, just enough so I could see her pretty good. Then I barred the back door and went into the main room to check the front door and the windows in there. I felt sure that everyone was gone, but I didn't want to take any chances. When I felt like the house was secure enough, I started to go back to her, but then I noticed how Sol was still sprawled out across the table. I went over to him and put him down on the floor and kind of straightened him out some. Then I went back into the bedroom. Maggie was lying on the bed. I could see her good in the dim light. She was on her back and was staring up at the ceiling with a kind of blank look on her face. I noticed again how gaunt her face was and how thin her lips. And her hair was thin and stringy. I let my eyes move down from her face, down the length of her body lying there. God, she was skinny. I could see the blue veins bulging under the white skin on her hands and feet. I could see every bone in her body, I thought. She looked wet and sticky all over. I remember thinking that she was covered with a mixture of her own and the sweat of four men. Her right arm was lying limp at her side, almost in the pool of blood left there on the dirty sheet by Butcher Knight. Her left hand was between her legs, the fingers tangled in the mat of wet, mouse-colored hair. The bottoms of her feet were dirty. I felt my upper lip twitch into a kind of snarl. I hated her.

"You make me sick," I said.

I hated myself, but I walked to the foot of the bed. When I did, her eyes opened a little wider, but there was no other change in her expression. She stretched her left arm out a little and started to rub the inside of her thigh, and she kept staring at the ceiling. I felt my face begin to burn, and I started breathing kind of heavy. I drew out my pistol and aimed it at her, and my hand was trembling.

"You brought the laws here, didn't you? You caused all this."

"Come here, Charlie," she said. "Get on top of me."

I dropped the gun on the foot of the bed and started to unbutton my shirt.

CHAPTER FORTY-THREE

Sol and French were dead. For all I knew, Butcher and Richard were too, and even if they weren't, I didn't have any idea where they would be. I wasn't really interested anyhow. What I realized was that I was glad to be shed of them. I wasn't like them. Or maybe I was. Maybe that was the trouble. Maybe I had found out, being with them, that I really was like that. Whatever it was, I didn't like it, and I had begun to realize that I didn't much like myself. I liked Mose, but he was gone, and I wasn't Mose, and I couldn't ever be Mose. I was Charlie Blackbird. Or was I Charles Black? Hellfire, I thought, I don't even know who in the hell I am. And I sure as hell didn't know where I was going.

I had left Maggie just the way I found her and started riding east first thing in the morning. Just east. I had no real destination. But after a while, I found myself riding in the woods where I used to hunt with Mose and Henry when we were kids. I remembered things that the three of us had done. I came across places where things had happened, and it seemed almost as if they had just happened, just before I came up on the place. And I started to feel real good, like I had gone back to those days. I was almost looking for Mose and Henry to show up just any minute, until I rode up over the little hill where Mose's cabin had been and I saw the black logs that had been lying there since the day they had blown the place up on him. And then the remembrance of that day came back to me, and I actually saw the smoke and the dust from the explosion once more, just like it was happening all over again. And I strained my eyes looking real hard into the smoke, and then I saw him again. It was happening all over. Mose came staggering out through that smoke, and he was all shot full of holes. It wasn't back when we were kids no more. It was all over. I felt my eyes fill up with tears, and the things I was looking at kind of faded away. I guess that I had got down off my horse while I was seeing all that, because when it all started to fade out, I just kind of sank down on the ground, and I sat there, and I cried like a baby. And then I got up on my knees, and I was looking up toward the sky through the tears.

"Mose," I said. "Mose, are you out there somewhere? Mose, what am I going to do? What the hell am I going to do?"

I slept the night up against the burned logs of Mose's cabin, and in the morning I got up and walked up the hill to the spot where Mose had buried Annie and their baby, and there were three graves there. The third one had to be Mose. I sat there for a while, I guess kind of paying my respects, and when I got up to leave, I don't know how it came to me, but when I got up to leave, I knew where I was going, although I didn't know exactly why. I took my horse down to the road and turned him loose. I figured someone would find him along the road before long. Then I headed east through the woods.

CHAPTER FORTY-FOUR

When I got close to the cabin, the dogs began to bark. I kept walking until I was right up in front. The dogs didn't come on up close to me. They ran around, and every now and then one of them would run up a little ways toward me, barking, and then run back closer to the house. I just stood there and let them bark. Pretty soon the door opened, and I could see that someone was looking out to find out who was outside.

"Charlie?"

"It's me, Sarah," I said.

Up until right then I hadn't known what to expect from her. I wasn't sure how she felt about me. I'm not sure why I went to her. But when she came out the door and started across the yard toward me, with her arms out and a big smile on her face, I knew that I'd made the right decision. And I remember thinking, as I watched her coming toward me, "How come I never noticed before how beautiful she is?"

The dogs were still barking, and she went right through the middle of them, kind of slapping at them as she came and scattering them in several different directions.

"*Hlesdi,*" she said to them. "*Winagi.*"

When she got out to where I was waiting, she hugged me to her. Then she stepped back to look at me.

"Charlie," she said. "How you doing?"

"Oh, I'm all right, Sarah," I said. "It's good to see you."

"Well, come on in. Whew. You all dirty and tired-looking. I bet you're hungry, too. Come on."

I went inside with her. Pretty soon the dogs stopped barking. She cooked me some eggs with wild onions and made some coffee. I thought that it was about the best food I'd had to eat in years. When I'd finished, I got cleaned up, and Sarah told me to sleep in her bed.

"Take off them dirty clothes," she said.

I did, and she took them from me. I went to bed naked, and I couldn't help thinking about how beautiful Sarah was and hoping that she would come to bed with me, but I was so tired that I couldn't even hold the thoughts in my head. Pretty soon, I was asleep. When I woke up the next morning, after a long, hard sleep, Sarah was already up and about. I had no idea where she had slept. My clothes were washed and hanging around to dry, and a fresh outfit was folded in a neat pile beside the bed. I could smell the coffee. That day, she went to gather more wild onions in the woods, and I went with her. In the evening, we went to the creek and caught a mess of crawdads. She cooked those for supper that night. I hadn't touched her since our first greeting in front of the house, and I don't really know how to explain it, but I felt better that day than I had felt since Mose had been gone. It felt good to be with her and to be doing those things with her. After we had finished supper, we went outside to sit in the yard. We got to talking about old times, about Mose and about Henry. We were both a little sad talking about those things, but at the same time it was pleasant just having somebody to talk to about it who understood and who felt the same way about it. After a while, we kind of ran out of things to say about the past, and we got quiet. Then Sarah looked at me with a sort of serious look on her face.

"Charlie," she said. "What are you doing with yourself now?"

"Well," I said, "I don't know. I mean, I really ain't too proud of myself right now, and I don't really know what to do or where to go."

"What's the matter, Charlie?"

I was comfortable with Sarah, and I trusted her. I hadn't really trusted anyone since Mose. And I had to tell somebody what it was that was bothering me, so I told her the whole story. I told her everything that had happened to me, everything I had done since Mose had been killed. I didn't leave out anything. Not how I'd deserted my pregnant wife and child, not the killings or the robberies, nothing. When I had finished, I was just kind of staring off into the woods.

"I can't find it, Sarah," I said. "Whatever the hell it is, I can't find it. Not without Mose. With him, it made sense, but it don't no other way. When I was with them other guys, I was just an outlaw. I don't know. I don't know what to do. The only thing I know is . . . well . . ."

"What, Charlie?"

"It feels better here with you than it has anywhere since them days with Mose."

She reached over and put a hand on me, and it sent a chill through my whole body. God, I wanted to reach over and pull her to me.

"I think I know," she said.

"What? You know what?"

"I think I know what it is you need."

"Well, what is it, then? Tell me."

"No. I can't tell you. It ain't that easy to tell. You stay here with me. Few days anyway. Okay? I think I know."

"You really mean that? You want me to stay?"

She smiled at me, and she was so beautiful in the moonlight that I wanted to cry.

"You stay. Come on now. Let's go inside."

Once we were back inside, she led me over to the bed. We stood facing each other, and we began to undress. When we had finished, she got onto the bed looking up at me. I lay down beside her and kissed her. It was the first time I'd ever kissed her, and with that first kiss, our bodies moved together. We made love and slept together that night, and it was the most beautiful night of my life.

CHAPTER FORTY-FIVE

We spent the next four days together like that. We gathered wild onions, mushrooms, berries. We fished. We swam in the creek. I hunted a little. We slept and made love together. We sometimes stayed in the house half the day, never getting dressed. And I was talking in Cherokee. Well, not really. What it was, Sarah was talking to me in Cherokee, and I was surprised at how much I could understand. The only time she'd use English was if I just couldn't get the meaning of what it was she was telling me. Then she'd explain it to me in English. And I started to talk in Cherokee whenever I could. So I was learning.

The fourth day I spent with Sarah was a Saturday. They had been wonderful days, the best, I guess, I had ever had in my life up until then, and I was grateful. I was almost happy, too. But somehow I was still bothered about what I should be doing, or where I should be going. Somehow I didn't think that this life, as great as it was, was all that she had meant when she told me that she knew what I needed. I asked her about it that Saturday.

"Wait until tonight," she said.

When the time came, we left the house together. It was late evening. We walked a few miles through the woods, and then I heard voices not far ahead of where we were at. I guessed that they were coming from our destination, but I didn't say anything. We walked on a little ways and came to a clearing. There were a number of Indian people gathered in the clearing, and I recognized it as a stomp ground. I had seen them before, although I was not at all familiar with what went on there. I felt nervous and out of place, but I walked on in among the people with Sarah.

" *'Siyo,* Sarah," said an old man.

" *'Siyo.*"

She seemed to know everybody there. I saw a few that I recognized, but I didn't really know them. Sarah introduced me to some of the people, and they were all friendly to me. I began to relax a little. For some time nothing happened. We just visited around with people. From time to time more people showed up. Some were sitting in small groups inside the little arbors which were built up around the edge of the grounds. I wondered if all those people who were seeing me there with Sarah thought I was a white man, and that thought embarrassed me. I didn't want them to think that. But nobody said anything or did anything to give me clues as to what they thought about me. Then Sarah got to talking to an old man. They were talking in Cherokee, and I couldn't hardly keep up with what they were saying, although I did catch a little bit every now and then, and I got the idea that she was telling him about me. One or the other of them would look over at me from time to time, and once, while Sarah was talking, I thought I heard Mose's Indian name. Pretty soon the old man wandered off to talk to someone else or to tend to something. Anyhow, that left me and Sarah alone for the time being. We sat down on a bench under an arbor.

"We were talking about you," she said.

"I thought so," I said, "but I wasn't going to say nothing about it."

"Could you understand us?"

"Not really. I thought that you were talking about me, and I thought I heard you say Mose's name once."

"Well," she said, "I did. I told him that you were with Mose that time, and how you and Mose were such good friends."

She looked at the ground. She seemed to be just a little bothered about something she was getting ready to say.

"He said," she told me, "that he thought you were a white man."

I must have looked hurt, maybe even a little mad.

"Hey," she said, "it's okay. I told him you're Cherokee, and when I told him about you and Mose, he was pretty impressed."

I felt a little better.

"Who is he, anyway?" I asked.

"He's Chief of this stomp ground."

Well, after a while the singing and dancing commenced, and it went on all night long. I didn't take part in it. I'd have felt like a fool, because it was the first time I had ever even been there. I just watched and listened. But I did stay up and awake the whole night through, and

I got a, well, I got a good feeling from being there. When the dancing was all over and done in the morning, some of the people left the area, and others just found themselves a spot to lie down in and go to sleep. Sarah said that we'd stay around. We slept under a big old tree just off the edge of the grounds. When Sarah woke me up, it was around noon. She led me back across the stomp ground to a place where people had laid out all kinds of food, and I ate until I was just about to bust open. Then we just waited around some more and visited some more. I didn't know what we were going to do next. Then I saw the Chief get up from his place by the fire, and he started to talk pretty loud in Cherokee. People started to gang up out on the ball field, and after some more preliminaries, the old Cherokee game of stickball was begun. The men were on one team and the women on the other. The men's team had to use the ballsticks, one in each hand, to throw the ball and try to hit the carved fish way up on top of the pole, but the women could just pick up the ball in their hands and throw it up there. Every time someone hit that fish, there was a lot of cheering. It looked like fun, and I wished that I could play. Sarah was playing, and she really looked pretty good to me, although I didn't hardly know what to watch for. There was a scorekeeper who was keeping score someway by marking on the ground with a stick, but I never did get the hang of how it was scored. Not that day. But it sure was fun watching, and I could tell how much those that were playing were enjoying it, and somehow it seemed like more than just fun. They were having fun, for sure, but it was more than that. When it was all over, me and Sarah walked back through the woods to her house. We didn't talk much on the way. When we got to the house, we undressed and got into bed. I kissed her.

"Charlie?" she said.

"What?"

"What do you think?"

"I want to go back again," I said. "I want to take part. I want to know what it's all about. I don't hardly know how to say this, but, well, I feel better than I've ever felt. I feel good. I, hell, I think I like myself."

She laughed a little.

"I'm glad for you," she said. "I thought it would be good for you."

"It was good for me. You were right about that, and I'll be grateful to you for it for the rest of my life. You've been really good to me, Sarah."

We were quiet for a minute. I kissed her again.

"But that ain't all," I said.

"What else, Charlie?"

"It ain't just the stomp dance. That was good for me, and I'm really glad you took me, but it ain't just that. It's these last four days I've spent with you, and it's all the things we've done together. It's, well, it's you, Sarah. Sarah?"

"Yes, Charlie?"

"Sarah, I don't want to lose all that. I don't want to lose what you've given me. I don't want to lose you. I want to stay here with you. Can I stay? Sarah, I . . . I love you."

CHAPTER FORTY-SIX

I don't think that anything that could ever happen could make me happier than the answer Sarah gave me that night. I resolved to stay with her from then on. I felt like I had finally found out where it was that I belonged. For the first time in my life, I felt like I had a place where I could stay. I was happy. I felt good. I was comfortable. I had a good woman. I loved her and she loved me. And I didn't have to worry anymore about whether I was Cherokee or white. But there was one more thing I wanted to do, and I told Sarah that next morning. I asked her to go with me. We got ready for a long walk, and we left right after breakfast. About a week earlier, I'd have been about half scared of what it was I was fixing to do, but when we finally walked up that hill, I was as calm as ever I could be. We were standing out in front of old Malachi Pathkiller's house. If he had heard us walking up, he didn't let on. The door was shut. There was no noise from inside. I waited just a little before I hollered.

"Hey, old man."

There was no answer, at least not as fast as I wanted it.

"Come out here, old man," I yelled.

The door opened, and Malachi stepped out of the darkness. If he was surprised to see me, he didn't let it show. He just walked on out. His withered arm was dangling at his side, and he was holding a carved walking stick in his good hand. I started on up the hill to meet him, but when I saw his stare, I stopped in my tracks. For a second I wasn't calm anymore. I was scared. I took a deep breath and reminded myself what I was up to.

"Old man," I said, "they've wiped out our government. They killed your two boys—my good friends. I tried two different paths for a while. Each one was wrong. I been lost, old man. This good woman—she knew your boys, too—she's helped me to find the right path, but I've got a lot to learn. I never did think you liked me. Because I'm a breed, maybe. I don't know. Well, you may not like me, but, old man, Mose and Henry was the only real friends I ever had. And I'm a Cherokee, even if I am a breed. And you may not like me, but damn it, you're the closest thing to an old man I got."

Malachi hadn't moved. His expression hadn't changed at all. I looked down and kind of shuffled my feet. Then I looked up at him again, but not straight in the eyes.

"Well," I went on, "you ain't got nothing here no more. You're here all by your lonesome, and the goddamn town is just down the road from you, so, damn it, we come to take you on back home with us."

"What do you want with me, Charlie Black?" said Malachi.

"It's Blackbird, Malachi," I said. "And what I want with you is, this good woman is going to have my kids, and they're going to be Chero-kee kids, and I don't want them to have to grow up as stupid as me."

Malachi stared at me a few seconds longer. He looked at Sarah. Then he slowly allowed a smile to creep onto his face. He motioned toward his door.

"I have a few things to get. Will you help me carry them? We better get started. We have a long ways to go, and I have a lot to teach you, so those kids won't grow up stupid like you."

Tears came into my eyes, but they came from a good feeling, and as I started toward the house, old Malachi put his good arm around my shoulder.

"Welcome home, son," he said.